Dr. Garzon accepts an invitation from Felix O'Neill to visit him at an isolated estate but he soon finds himself involved with child murder in a house of fear. The estate is owned by O'Neill's uncle, an eccentric professor who is surrounded by his obsequious amanuensis, an oriental governess, strange children, cowled monks and nocturnal intruders.

LIFE OF DREW CARSON

Sam Drew Carson was born in the North of Ireland and educated there at Wellington College and the Ulster Polytechnic. He completed his education in the USA at New Mexico Highlands University and the University of Arkansas and has traveled widely in North America, around the Atlantic and in Europe.

Drew worked as a seaman and fish-gutter in Vestmannaeyjar off the coast of Iceland. He lived and worked in the Irish and Western Isles Gaeltachts and was married in Welsh-speaking Carmarthen after which he honeymooned in Belfast. He has told his stories, composed and sung his songs, seeking storylines in Bristol and the English Westcountry. Drew has also lived and written in Nashville, Tennessee, in the wooded hills of Mid-America and from the Appalachians to the Ozarks. This was the culture that gave rise to the now worldwide Scotch-Irish country music.

In the USA, he also worked beside the bayous of the French-speaking Cajuns in the South and among the Western Spanish-speaking Navajos, Apaches and Pueblos of the Sangre de Cristo Mountains in New Mexico.

Drew has sailed far into the seas of old Gaelic and Oriental legend. After many years searching for inspiration for story and music, the author is still traveling and writing.

BOOKS BY DREW CARSON

SAGA OF TSUNAMI –
the Trilogy, 2nd edition
ISBN: 978-0-9561435-1-8

ZENISUB –
Fun and Games in Businezz
ISBN: 978-0-9561435-2-5

GOOD FOR A LAUGH –
Six Funny Playscripts for Amateurs
ISBN: 978-0-9561435-3-2

HOME WITH A GOOD COMPANION –
Amateur Pantomime Scripts for a Merry Winter
ISBN: 978-0-9561435-4-9

BACK TO THE GOOD OLD DAYS –
Miracle Plays of Sunlight and Shadow
ISBN: 978-0-9561435-5-6

CLASSIC EUROPEAN LYRICS –
Translated from the Gaelic, the French and Spanish
ISBN: 978-0-9561435-6-3

COMMONWEALTH –
An Introduction to Business Economics
ISBN: 978-0-9561435-7-0

MISSING PERSONS –
Detective Felix O'Neill in a Crime Adventure
ISBN: 978-0-9561435-8-7

WEREWOLF MURDERS –
Detective Felix O'Neill in a Crime Adventure
ISBN: 978-0-9561435-9-4

ORIENTAL GOVERNESS –
Detective Felix O'Neill in a Crime Adventure
ISBN: 978-1-908184-00-9

Oriental Governess

Detective Felix O'Neill in a Crime Adventure

DREW CARSON

Order from: https://www.createspace.com/3882460

Legals

ISBN: 978-1-908184-00-9

MAIN CHARACTERS

Dr. Arturo Garzon - A mature doctor specializing in healthics.

Mr. Felix O'Neill - O'Neill is a former accountant and inventor who is working independently to develop an innovative approach to the solving of serious crimes based on the logic of auditing and statistical method.

Dr. Conn O'Neill - The elderly great-uncle of Felix O'Neill. Dr. Conn is putting together a comprehensive work of reference on eastern and natural remedies.

Heronius Plumet - A secretary skilled in eastern languages and assisting Dr. Conn O'Neill in compiling his great work on oriental medicine.

Miss Songana - An oriental governess of uncertain age. She lives in the O'Neill mansion where she teaches the two young children. She is skilled in the French and Spanish languages, eastern culture and other civilized accomplishments.

Cormac and Doreen - Two child cousins of Felix O'Neill.

Sadie and Maisie the Housemaids and Moira the Cook - Servants in the O'Neill mansion.

An Indian Fakir - A figure of fun and some mystery.

Harry - A xenophobic manservant, old-fashioned and weak.

Juan Gallegos - The Hispanic owner of a fine hostelry, close by the old O'Neill family estate – a place where O'Neill and Garzon like to dine.

A Friar - A lay brother who presents a warning of weird events to come.

TABLE OF CONTENTS

CHAPTER ONE

An Invitation from Mr. O'Neill

Dr. Garzon, completing research into healthics, receives an invitation from Felix O'Neill to visit an old O'Neill family mansion. O'Neill feels isolated among the mixed bunch of companions and distant relatives.

I have received over the years many requests to recount my greatest adventure with Felix O'Neill. So far I have refrained from answering these requests in order to observe the well established conventions of discretion and confidentiality.

However, with the passing of so many years such confidences, particularly as regards my own weaknesses, become less personal and more a matter of history and tales well told.

I was a mature researcher at the time, so perhaps my readers will forgive my pitiful limitations in view of the later friendship and support which I was privileged to give to Mr. O'Neill. Therefore, the story that follows is the only accurate account of our greatest case together.

I have carefully considered the sympathy and encouragement and the lack of any nefarious criticism on the part of the many admirers of Mr. O'Neill. I have also thought about the very friendly early response of readers to my literary proposals concerning the greatest achievement of the former accountant now a great detective. These have all eventually prevailed upon me to tell of Felix O'Neill's greatest case.

Indeed, it appears to be a matter of great interest to some how my professional relationship eventually developed with Mr. Felix O'Neill.

It is not generally known that O'Neill's greatest case was the original voluntary help which he gladly gave for the benefit of his country cousins in the Celtcountry. At that time they were in the direst peril in the case of the oriental governess.

It is strange how coincidence or mere chance or even necessity often sets us out on our various roads of destiny in this life. Mr. O'Neill was in fact destined to be a detective or to perish in the flames of an old country mansion. It was a case of destroy or be destroyed; analyze or be annihilated. Life and the practice of healthics often presents these stark choices. This was Felix O'Neill's finest professional case undertaken for reasons of scientific challenge after the formulation of his system of logical forensics based on his methodical and legal studies in auditing.

I will now tell the story of O'Neill's encounter with a dangerous mystery. It all happened just before the completion of my post-doctoral research in healthics and therefore lead up to my maritime, seagoing service in the cause of our great eastern empire. Before this Mr. O'Neill and I had been in proximate digs at our old college town of Oldseaside.

Although O'Neill was essentially a solitary researcher, he had demonstrated some interesting experiments to his fellow accountants during our informal self-study hours in various laboratories. In this way O'Neill and I had come to be acquainted.

It was there, many years later, that Mr. O'Neill and I were to share digs on the Promenade at Oldseaside. But enough of these reminiscences.

At any rate, here is O'Neill's letter to me which lead to solving this mystery. I take it from my desk and copy it as it stands addressed to Dr. Garzon. It begins:

My Dear Garzon,

If you knew my utter loneliness and complete weariness I am sure you would have pity upon me and come down to share my solitude. You have often made vague promises of visiting Fiersley and having a look at our magnificent Celtcountry Peaks. What time would suit you better than the present? You still have about three months before your scheduled date for the completion of your articles. The long journey would be repaid by the warm dry weather here, unlike the cool April showers you may expect in your part of the country.

Of course, I understand that you are hard at work but you can read just as well here as at the School of Healthics. Pack up your books like a good fellow and come along. We have a snug little suite of rooms, fully plumbed and with writing-desk and armchair which will just do for your research. Let me know when we may expect you.

When I say that I am lonely, I do not mean that there is any lack of people in the house. On the contrary we form rather a large household. First and foremost comes my learned but highly eccentric and garrulous great Uncle Conn, shuffling about in his riding boots. A Doctor of Philosophy with a thesis on the efficacy of eastern healthics, he is intently researching and compiling a great collection of oriental remedies. I think I told you when last we met how his great lifework would be of interest to you in your present studies.

His enthusiasm for the subject of eastern healthics has now attained such a pitch that he has hired an editor cum secretary whose sole duty it is to copy down, set in order and lavishly praise my uncle's exotic descriptions. This fellow is named Heronius Plumet. He is an expert in oriental languages and I view him as more than a little sinister but what should one expect from a student of Mandarin, Hindi, and Urdu? 'Much learning hath made him mad,' might be my conspectus for either master or servant.

So be sure to take a break or two from your own research having due respect for the inevitable effect of higher education upon the human brain.

At any rate Plumet has become as necessary to the old doctor as pen or foolscap paper.

Then we have the two surviving children of my late great Uncle Shane. These two children had been adopted by great Uncle Conn. They have never been quite the same since their sister was recently found inexplicably dead in the garden so their strange behavior along with their awkward and shy manners are all quite understandable.

Such a tragedy is enough to make anyone stultified and glazed but no doubt they will recover in time, helped by the kindness of their oriental governess - a beautiful mature lady with a touch of eastern mystery in her makeup. One of her earlier charges also suffered a fatal attack so that she is very empathetic to the children's tragic situation. Uncle Conn has welcomed her as complementary to his research.

Can you begin to see why I must have some compatible company? Everyone here is an enigma. I can't take it anymore, Garzon. Even the servants, three maidservants and the old groom, are always fearfully and guiltily lurking around. They have reported seeing weird visions of oriental ghosts in the nighttime and have been suspected of lying.

So you see, we have quite a little world of our own in this out of the way corner. For all that, my dear Garzon, I long for a familiar face and for a congenial companion. I am deep in photographic invention myself so I won't interrupt your studies too much. Please write by return to your isolated friend.

Felix O'Neill.

At the time I received this letter I was in lodgings near the School of Healthics in Oldseaside and was working hard on my post-doctoral research. O'Neill and I had been close friends since we first attended college. This was before O'Neill's sudden departure to engage in his own brilliant independent studies in the advanced sciences, including the secret sciences of ancient and future times. Certainly I would have dearly liked to see O'Neill again. On the other hand, I was rather afraid that in spite of his assurances, my research might suffer by the long journey and the new surroundings. It is always difficult to adjust to any kind of change even if it is a change for the better.

I pictured to myself the eccentric old professor, the obsequious editor, the stylish oriental governess, the difficult children, the trembling, ancient servants and I came to the conclusion that when we were all cooped together in one country house there would be very little time for quiet reading. At the end of two days' cogitation I had almost made up my mind to refuse the invitation when I received another letter from the Celtcountry even more pressing than the first. Little did I realize that this letter was to convince me to accept the invitation. My friend O'Neill wrote:

We expect to hear from you by every post and there is never a knock that I do not think is a telegram announcing your train. Your suite is all ready and I think you will find it comfortable. Uncle Conn bids me say how very happy he will be to see you. He would have written but he is absorbed in his great compendium of eastern cures and he spends his day researching old documents and interpreting them with help from the oriental governess and the secretary-editor chap who lurks behind him like the graypower behind the throne, his notebook and pencil jotting down the English translations of the old professor's finds. Dr. Conn O'Neill of course can sometimes make a pretty good, though not exact, guess as to the meaning of these old manuscripts.

By the way, the dark governess is a real first-class help with research and translations. She often studies from a book of wisdom written in some old eastern language. It is strange to see her poring over the leaves by the light of an antique lamp that is supposedly sacred to some or other group of scholars. She is the child of an Anglo lady and an eastern healtharian practitioner who was killed in the mutiny while supporting the fighting against us. His estates being seized, his daughter was brought to this country by her mother. Eventually she answered uncle's advertisement for a governess. Uncle Conn, being no shrinking violet, naturally referred to his great life's work as a collector of eastern healthics. Her expertise in such matters got her the job as much as her love of children and suitability as a governess.

So you can see that we are all well into the study of science and in particular the science of healthics. Therefore you will feel quite at home here. Think of what you will learn in an atmosphere that's really conducive to research. So my dear chap do not hesitate a minute longer but come at once for I absolutely demand the opportunity to be once again your friend and host.

Your sincere fellow researcher,

Felix O'Neill

There was no resisting the importunity of my old comrade. So with only a few inward grumbles I hastily packed up my books, jars, specimens and some surgical instruments, telegraphed a reply overnight and left Oldseaside for the Celtcountry first thing the next morning.

I well remember that it was a miserable day and the journey required a transfer at the Interchange. It seemed to be an interminable one as I sat huddled up in a corner of the draughty carriage, revolving in my mind many problems of naturopathy and healthics. I had been advised that the little wayside station of Fiersley, near Seaview, was the nearest to my destination and it was there that I alighted.

CHAPTER TWO
My Friend Mr. O'Neill

Felix O'Neill meets Dr. Garzon at the train and, driving to the O'Neill estate, describes the strange assortment of characters living at the old hall.

At about the same time as I arrived at the station Felix O'Neill, dressed in a tweed cape and matching robinhood hat, came dashing down the country road in a high dogcart. My hawkish friend waved his whip enthusiastically at the sight of me and pulling up his horse with a jerk sprang out and on to the platform.

O'Neill showed his lean and energetic aristocratic background. As usual, he wore a carnation in the top buttonhole of his superb jacket. And as always, his brilliant brain looked out at the world through his sharp blue-gray eyes, yet showed in his speech little trace of his Irish origins. Rather, O'Neill spoke the Queen's English firmly and clearly with no trace of any Westcountry or other accent.

"My dear Garzon," he cried, "I'm so delighted to see you. It's so kind of you to come."

He wrung my hand until my arm ached then carefully placed my three bags in the back of the trap, mindful of the implements and jars that he knew must be therein.

"I'm afraid you'll find me very bad company now that I am here," I answered. "I am up to my ears in work."

"Of course, of course," he said, in his good-humored way. "I had reckoned on as much. We'll have time for a crack at the rabbits for all that. It's a longish drive and you must be bitterly cold. So let's start for home at once."

We climbed into the trap and rattled off along the bumpy and dusty road at a brisk canter.

"Life is like a country road with all ups and downs," smiled O'Neill.

"We've just got to take the rough with the smooth," I added cheerfully.

"I think you'll like your suite of rooms - bed-sitting room, toilet and bathroom all to yourself," my friend remarked. "You'll soon find yourself at home. You know it's not often that I visit Seaview House since I came here as a boy but I could not refuse my great uncle's generous offer of free rooms for my experiments.

"As a remote cousin, I have always been astonished at my uncle's generosity to me and to others whom he regards as worthy of encouragement. He is a kind, good country squire at heart with a belief that all should be treated fairly. Merit not blood is his belief. That's why Plumet and I are in his good books at present.

"Anyway, I am only just beginning to settle down and get my laboratory into working order for the development of a new camera. This would be a camera with a full developing, printing and enlarging system which is my ultimate focus - no pun intended, dear chap."

He glanced sideways at me.

I smiled, "You're in great form these days, O'Neill. I did like your little joke about the inevitable effect of higher education on the human brain. You know, dear fellow, there's many a true word spoken in jest. It is a fact that my poor brain is nearly scrambled with analysis. It says in the good book somewhere that too much study is a weariness to the flesh, true words."

"I know exactly how you feel, Garzon. That's why I think you'll enjoy this change of scenery and climate. Look over there."

He indicated with his whip a steep pointed high hill.

"That's Fiersley Peak, the scene of a druidic ceremony, a 'pagan meet' in local dialect, some years back. The perpetrators were caught, fined and briefly jailed but rumors persist that the old religion still survives underground. Have you noticed a few of those chaps around?"

I nodded as two tall, cowled friars in dark gray robes strolled towards us, giving us the sign of the cross as a traveling blessing and nodding in a friendly but somewhat solemn and inscrutable manner.

"Indeed O'Neill, those are certainly very orthodox chaps and little druidism will get by them in a hurry, I'll warrant."

"Perhaps so Garzon but things are not always as they appear. However, they are monks from Bleakley Abbey quite nearby and they do have a good reputation locally.

"So does the landlord of the local inn. By the way, he is a renowned Hispanic cook and baker known as Juan Gallegos. As you know, I am partly of Hispanic descent on the female side so that Hispanic cuisine means down-home to O'Neill. When your research is completed we must eat at Juan's Inn. I've known Juan since I was a child visiting my uncle here. Gallegos is a great character."

I remarked that the terrain was bleak and strewn with huge gray granite boulders.

"And treacherous mires too Garzon. Remember that, if you go walking. One of us at the house will be sure to go with you when you feel like a trek.

"By the way, that peak is Blackfiend Beacon over twelve hundred feet high and said to be named after the ghost of a great black dog with fiery sulfurous breath. These dogs are feared to be possessed by the souls of undead children and are known as fiendhounds in localese, meaning they are cunning and savage. Such hounds have been seen in the area occasionally over a period of hundreds of years.

"Yes, long since, there have even been many rumors of the Grayreaper and his manhounds - fierce human heads that howl and wail on canine bodies."

"Who is the Grayreaper?" I asked.

"Satan," replied O'Neill briskly. "Then Ogre Peak, over that away, is said to be a wicked giant turned into a granite peak by a Celtic magician."

I laughed, "O'Neill, this is a jolly place for real entertainment. There's a pub run by a skilled Hispanic baker and cook. Giants and ghost dogs. I say what fun. Any chance of an escaped convict from the lunatic prison over by the old castle?"

"Don't laugh too much, old boy. Be careful. There's an undercurrent of things evil and sinister in these parts and something that I cannot quite put my finger on. I hesitate to believe, of course, in such unscientific phenomenons as phantom canines or petrified giants but I do sense some unholy underpinnings in these parts, menacing and uncanny. So do take care, there's a good chap."

I assured my friend, "I'm always a cautious fellow O'Neill, as you know, but I'll be especially wary among the err Celtic mists. I take it the locals don't take kindly to strangers, O'Neill?"

"Right on Garzon. They are especially wary of the Orientals whom Uncle Conn brings here at times. But any stranger, of any complexion, is an object of suspicion among the local xenophobiacs who are mostly illiterate loafers with nothing better to do."

O'Neill looked puzzled, "Or are they? How do they find a living? At any rate the educated and professional groups, as well as the local gentry, are really more of Uncle Conn's disposition so that our oriental governess has been fairly well received. Of course," and here O'Neill glanced at me sideways, "she is an extremely beautiful, cultured and intelligent lady."

"Oh really, O'Neill? I'm looking forward to meeting her." I replied unwarily.

"Quite so," nodded O'Neill, "You'll be glad you joined us then."

"The whole scene begins to interest me, O'Neill, I must confess. There are age-old mysteries in the very air here, as you tell it, and mysteries are the spice of life."

"Yes," agreed O'Neill, "they surely are."

Neither of us at that point knew just how true these casual statements were to prove. Literally, lives would depend on the solving of mysteries by O'Neill, including his life and mine.

"By the way, Garzon," added O'Neill, "those dark hooded monks are liable to turn up anywhere at anytime of the day or night. Only the other night I saw two such cowled and robed figures cross our lawn at three in the morning when I was still burning the midnight oil in my lab."

"Do you mean to say they showed up without permission, O'Neill?"

"They cannot trespass," O'Neill assured me. "An old baronial charter gives them permission to walk and bless the land all over the barony. I don't really know if nowadays this is a good work of the church or a patrol against druids and bardic celebrants but it does occur to me that anyone could disguise themselves in cowl and robe pretty easily."

"Including those up to no good eh, O'Neill?"

"Exactly, my dear Garzon."

At this point our road ran over a succession of low bleak hills which were devoid of all vegetation save a few scattered whin bushes and a thin covering of stiff wiry grass which gave nourishment to a scattered flock of lean, hungry-looking sheep. Alternately, we dipped down into a hollow or rose up to the summit of a little brae from which we could see the road winding as a thin white track over successive hills beyond.

Every here and there the monotony of the landscape was broken by the jagged scarps known locally as peaks where the gray under-rock peeped grimly out as though nature had been sorely wounded until her gaunt bones protruded through their covering. In the distance lay a range of mountains with one great peak shooting up from amongst them, coquettishly draped in a wreath of clouds which reflected the ruddy light of the setting sun.

"That's Fiersley Peak again," my companion said indicating the mountain with his whip, "and those are the Celtic Hills. You won't find a wilder or a bleaker place in all the Western World. Yet the Celtcountry is known as home to the bravest of the brave."

"Yes, one of the lands of my remote Scots ancestors," I reminded my friend.

"Exactly Garzon and each has its own variant of language, books, authors, artists and sense of loyalty. In other words, its own coherent culture. As you know, I have the greatest admiration for the Celtic civilizations. Though you are not much into social sciences, old chap, I'm sure that you will soon come to love the stories and poems of the old Celts."

I concurred, "I am sure you are right. I love the tales of King Arthur and his knights of the round table. I'm proud to know that we are all part of the same great worldwide empire. We are all a mixture of Vikings and Gaels."

O'Neill smiled, nodded and pointed his whip at the main gate.

"This is the end of your long journey. Just jump down old fellow and open the gate."

CHAPTER THREE
A Warm Welcome

Dr. Garzon is welcomed by Felix O'Neill's ancient and witty great Uncle Conn who is a writer and researcher of ancient cures. Garzon meets other odd denizens at the estate such as Heronius Plumet the obsequious secretary of the old uncle.

We had pulled up at a place where a long moss-grown wall ran parallel to the road. It was broken by a dilapidated iron gate flanked by two pillars. On the summit of these were stone devices which appeared to represent some heraldic animal. The sea winds and rains had reduced the pillars to shapeless blocks.

A cottage which served as a lodge stood on one side. I pushed the gate open and we drove up a long, winding avenue, grass-grown and uneven but lined by magnificent oaks which shot their branches so thickly over us that the evening twilight deepened suddenly into darkness.

"I'm afraid our avenue won't impress you much," O'Neill said, with a laugh. "It's one of the old man's whims to let nature have her way as much as possible. The Tudor gate lodge there is timbered and flowered with sweet smells from the fields and trees. Only Plumet, the secretary, is ever allowed to sleep there for his health's sake. A privileged fellow as you'll soon find out. Here we are at last at Seaview."

As he spoke, we swung around a curve in the avenue marked by a patriarchal oak which towered high above the others. Suddenly we came upon a great old gray-stoned house with a lawn in front of it.

The house was on a cliff and faced south. It was high above and overlooking the magnificent sea. There were two wings, east and west.

The west wing, I was to discover later, was for guest and family quarters and was made up of several suites each with sitting room, bedroom and bathroom. This wing was connected to the main block by a rambling stone annex.

The only occupants of the west wing were Uncle Conn, Plumet, the governess and the children. Felix and I were to have our own separate suites in the west wing.

I was to discover that these residential suites had been well modernized and plumbed to a high standard, as O'Neill had promised. As proved important later, all suites had locks for the safety and privacy of the occupants.

In the center stood the main building housing the dining rooms, drawing rooms, a magnificent ballroom and hospitality hall with kitchens to the rear.

The east wing contained the manual servants quarters with stables and stores and outbuildings located on the periphery. This was also connected to the main building by an uneven stone structure.

When we arrived, the lower part of the building was all in shadow but up at the top a row of bloodshot windows squinted out at the setting sun.

At the sound of the wheels, a very old man in livery staggered out and seized the horse's head when we pulled up.

"You can put her up, Harry," my friend said as we jumped down.

Then turning away, "Garzon, let me introduce you to my great uncle Dr. Conn O'Neill."

"How d'ye do? How d'ye do?" cried a wheezy cracked voice and looking up I saw a little red-faced old man who was standing waiting for us on the porch. He wore a white sun helmet on his head after the fashion of the jungle and desert explorers. This huge hat was matched by a white leather-belted jacket, Bermuda shorts and riding boots. These contrasted so strangely with his white sunless skin, hands and knees that he looked for all the world like a figure in a museum designed to depict an imperial warrior of times past.

"How are you Dr. Conn?" I asked.

"Well, with age comes wisdom. The older I get the more I understand the full power of the earth's gravitational pull," replied the old man.

"Oh really, sir?" I asked seriously. "Is that your field of research, Doctor?"

The old man smiled and shook his head wryly.

"No, I'll talk about my research later, old chap."

He flexed his arms and legs slightly.

"No, I just feel the force of gravity more than ever nowadays, especially here and there when I walk. You know I'm a-falling apart and a shaking bagabones. I need to be grabbed by the neck and slammed away into some obscure cupboard to become a family skeleton."

He laughed loudly and shook my hand heartily.

"Any friend of Felix is a friend of mine. You are most welcome, dear fellow.

"You must be tired sir. Yes and cold sir," he said in a warm and bright tone, as he shook me by the hand.

"We must be hospitable to you. We must indeed. Hospitality is one of the great eastern virtues which we also should recapture and respect."

He scratched his head, "Let me see now, what is that Mongolian proverb?"

"A sheltered traveler may bring healing from afar," said a voice behind him and a tall, long-visaged man in black suit and white collar stepped forward into the circle of light which was thrown by the lamp above the porch.

Dr. Conn beamed at the interruption. Felix O'Neill introduced the tall man as Plumet. I remember that Plumet's hand, as I shook it, was cold and unpleasantly clammy. Looking at him closely I could see that he was not a priest or cleric of any kind but merely someone who cultivated the appearance of such.

This ceremony over, my lean and wiry friend O'Neill picked up the two largest of my suitcases as though they were balloons and led me towards my suite of rooms, with old Harry blowing and puffing and dragging my third bag along the floor. Harry almost tripped over a fire bucket and, tired as I was, I had to take my bag from him and dismiss him. So as not to embarrass the old retainer, I muttered my thanks to him and said something tactful about fearing for my jars and specimens, though in fact these heavy items were in the bags so casually carried ahead by O'Neill. I noted that the dolichomorphic Plumet had not offered to help, despite his station as a servant.

At any rate, we passed through many passages and corridors connected by old fashioned and irregular staircases. As we did, I noticed as I passed the thickness of the walls and the strange slants, cornices and angles of the ceilings, suggestive of mysterious spaces above.

There were several suites of chambers among all the nooks and crannies in the west wing. The chambers set apart for me were a cheery little sanctum with a crackling coal fire and a bookcase well-stocked with healtharian reference books. Indeed, the shelves were lined with dictionaries of all the healtharian sciences from herbology and homeopathy to psychology and hypnotherapy. Numerous other books of oriental remedies had been furnished with the compliments of Dr. Conn O'Neill.

I expressed my satisfaction to my friend Felix. He nodded.

"Not neglecting prayer and music therapy, dietology, osteopathy, physiology and acupuncture," I added. "I see the book there that I need most. There it is, that huge volume on Cognicology and Learning Theory."

O'Neill pointed to Breathonics. "Don't forget your fresh air and walking and deep breathing, old boy.

"My uncle is very well equipped to help you in any aspect of your research. Otherwise I would have hesitated to send for you."

I thanked O'Neill and began to think, as I pulled on my slippers, that I might have done worse after all than to accept this Celtcountry invitation from my good friend. Little did I realize how much this invitation was to mean to both of us.

CHAPTER FOUR
A Menage of Healthics

As Garzon dines with the humorous uncle and the family, they all discuss alternative healthics and oriental remedies. The two young children, remote cousins of Felix, prove to be precocious and witty.

When we descended to the dining-room, the rest of the household had already assembled for dinner around one of the smaller tables.

Uncle Conn O'Neill whom I shall generally refer to as Dr. Conn, still wearing his white sun helmet, sat at the head of the table. At the place of honor on his right sat the stiffly clerical and formal amanuensis, next to whom I was seated. Facing Dr. Conn and to my diagonal right was his nephew and of course my friend Felix whom I usually refer to simply as O'Neill.

On the left of Dr. Conn sat a very dark complexioned and gracefully long-necked lady with black hair and fine, sad eyes who was introduced to me as Miss Songana. She was very easy to look at, absolutely dressed to kill in a beautiful silk gown.

Beside her and just opposite me were two pretty but worried-looking children,

Cormac, a boy and Doreen, a girl, who were evidently the beautiful lady's charges.

Dr. Conn shrewdly glanced at the children and then, in a clear attempt to cheer them up, he lifted his white sun helmet and replaced it quickly, briefly revealing a bald pate.

"Don't you two children imagine for one minute that I'm as bald as you think. Why goodness heavens me only this morning I counted twenty seven little fine hairs on the very top of my head and that's three more than I counted before I started using this hair restorer. You see, it really does work."

He held up his tiny glass of wine so that it sparkled in the candlelight and then downed it drastically with one or two quick gulps. The children tee-heed evasively and hid their faces behind their hands as they giggled at each other.

The children both shared a vague family resemblance to their cousin Felix and their Uncle Conn.

As for Miss Songana, I knew that she was half Anglo but I could not even guess from what part of our great eastern empire her father might have come - India, China, Mongolia, East Africa or the Holy Land perhaps but more likely somewhere like

Malaya or Burma I thought.

I can almost fancy now that I still see the yellow glare of the great oil lamp throwing Rembrandt-like lights and shades upon the ring of faces, some of which were soon to have so strange an interest for me.

On the whole it was a long pleasant meal, even apart from the excellence of the viands and the fact that the long journey had sharpened my appetite.

Uncle Conn overflowed with anecdote and quotation, delighted to have found a new listener. Neither Miss Songana nor the children spoke a great deal.

Plumet rattled off quite a bit and all that he said bespoke an arrogantly witty as well as a formally educated man but certainly no great genius.

As to Felix O'Neill and I, we had so much in hand of reminiscences and subsequent events that we were compelled to postpone our talk until after dinner or risk boring the company to tears.

However, Dr. Conn was the life and soul of the party and there were one or two brief incidents during the meal which I do recall even now with some slight personal vexation.

For example, at one point Dr. Conn inquired politely if I had had a good journey.

"Well, from the Interchange to here was pretty good," I answered. "The weather here is fairly mild at the moment."

"But how then was the long leg of your journey?" asked Dr. Conn.

"From Oldseaside to the Interchange was freezing. In fact, very draughty almost the whole way," I replied. "Still, you've got to expect as much at this time of the year."

"Pity you just missed the express," commented O'Neill.

"Yes," nodded Dr. Conn, "if only you had come down on an express it would have been much warmer." Dr. Conn shook his head in commiseration.

I gazed from Dr. Conn to O'Neill in blank amazement.

"How did you know that I just missed the express? I didn't mention it. And you've no idea how long I may have waited in the Interchange."

"Principles of blood pressure." Dr. Conn assured me cryptically as he attacked the flaky red steak with a knife and fork.

"I'm afraid I don't quite follow." I said as I shook my head in mystification.

"Felix you explain, there's a good chap," muttered Dr. Conn, evidently more interested in gulping down a large helping of steak and swilling down some good

Celtcountry cider.

"Certainly Uncle," O'Neill responded brightly. "You see, my dear Garzon, it's as clear as sunbeams. At this time of year it's quite shivery in most places so that passengers sitting on the express, once their blood pressure has settled down, would never dream of opening a carriage window.

"But the regular train that you no doubt took, stopping at almost every station, would attract new passengers as seats were vacated. Each new traveler's blood would be pounding from the effort of boarding with suitcases or even rushing or running in some instances. The result is a steady stream of puffing and huffing newcomers who invariably insist on opening the window until their raised blood pressure calms down. You must have noticed the pattern. That's why your journey was draughty most but not all of the time. As for your trying to catch the express, well that's only common sense for one setting out on a long journey."

"Of course, of course," I mumbled.

In truth, I felt quite embarrassed at not having understood anything as very basic and straightforward as blood pressure. After all, I was supposed to be an expert on healthics.

Seeing my spluttering, Dr. Conn kindly changed the subject. Indeed, he was as nice as ninepence. He meant well. However, for me it was a case of out of the frying pan into the fire.

At this point Dr. Conn had been eating too fast. He coughed, spluttered a little and shook his head. "Oh shut up, shut up, you dottering old fool, you imbecile," he admonished himself furiously.

"Disgusting old age," he screamed at himself. "Hawking, retching, catarrhing and spitting. How vile can a filthy old man get," he wailed with mock self hatred. "I need a good Turkish bath, I do."

The children giggled and covered their laughter with polite hands and I noticed that Miss Songana did not suppress them but merely smiled.

All laughed but some uneasily as though afraid of offending the old man by agreeing with him. To demur would have been to take it all too seriously.

At this point Dr. Conn leaned over and patted my shoulder.

"I'm so glad to have you here, Garzon. A healtharian expert is assured of an honored place here, I can tell you. Just recently Felix remarked to me how helpful it would be to his old friend Garzon to spend a few weeks here. Now here you are and as welcome as the spring. Ha, Ha. Tell me, is your research directed towards allopathy or homeopathy, my dear chap?"

I was somewhat caught out by his sudden semantic query. However, I quickly recovered my poise as I recalled that one of my former colleagues in a fit of professional excitement had once praised homeopathy at some length.

"Oh yes, Dr. Conn, I err do research in the field of allopathy or perhaps it's homeopathy. I'm not quite sure. The books do not always make it clear," I replied carefully, though of course I understood his meaning in a general sense.

My host shook his head sadly and then in a tone of commiseration as one offering condolences to a bereaved friend, "I feared as much. Many books and articles have been written by underqualified lecturers, no doubt. All college lecturers should have Ph.Ds in their field as well as extensive publications."

"Still," said Dr. Conn as he continued to warmly pat my shoulder, "my own research specialty is oriental treatments including homeopathic healthics and remedies. Of course, I am not a clinical practitioner, rather the author of books and short monographs on the subject."

Then he pointed towards the oriental governess and the translator secretary, "At the moment I have the help of these good folks in compiling my great reference book, a virtual panorama, covering the entire field of eastern cures. It will be the first of its kind you may be interested to know.

"Anyhow as I was saying," continued Dr. Conn cheerfully, "allopathy is just an aggressive attack on the mere symptoms of a sickness. It attacks the symptoms in all ways at any cost to the patient."

He stabbed the air with knife and fork and growled dramatically.

"Hit those mean, nasty symptoms and hit 'em hard, that's a rugby player's philosophy, very unsubtle. Cut it off or electrocute it or dose it away with crude drugs. Rake it out with a knife. Squeeze it. Pour somebody else's blood into it. Saw through the bone to get at it, remove the skull and then slash it out. Rip it away. I do wonder how any poor body survives at all in our hospitals and clinics.

"Eastern healthics is more subtle. It says, restore the wholeness to the person and don't just attack the sickness. Sickness is cunning and evasive. It will only slink away and hide somewhere only to reappear somewhere else."

I laughed at Dr. Conn's satirical attack on modern western healthics.

"My goodness, you would go down well in the younger healtharian student's dorm get-togethers," I cried. "I know that they would appreciate all that doctor bashing."

"Of course, Dr. Conn," said Plumet, jumping on the bandwagon, "there is a satirical way to look at anything including acupuncture, acupressure, food withdrawal, aromatherapy, hydrotherapy, herbalism or manual therapy. Why, my goodness, all that could be characterized as stick pins or fingers in the patients, starve 'em, half-drown 'em, handbash on 'em, stink 'em out. Make 'em drink weed water."

Uncle Conn loved it. "Yes of course, it all depends on the language that you use, doesn't it?"

It was obvious that he was clearly impressed with Plumet's wit which, to be fair, was really quite keen at times.

After this Felix O'Neill commented favorably on homeopathy as a lifelong inquirer into unorthodox ideas.

"It's not quackery," he said, "it's opposed by some doctors because it sells fewer expensive drugs. There is a deep mystery about homeopathy that has never been solved. Although I believe it is connected with immunization but after, not before, the onset of the disease.

"In this sense homeopathy is close to the mechanisms of prevention and it is unorthodox because it doesn't support expensive orthodox cures. It doesn't enrich its practitioners. It is healthics for the poor. Drugs are expensive and usually transfer the sickness from one part of the body to another, sometimes severely."

Dr. Conn interposed, "Yes I prefer to say new or unorthodox rather than quack. I myself have found that what is feared or not understood is often castigated as quackery. I am at present trying to research very unusual remedies from the east. I'm not qualified in clinical practice so I am a quack myself. At my next visit to the King of Arms, I will put a duck on my armorial bearing with the motto, Quack, Quack."

Plumet addressed me personally and condescendingly, "Try to understand Dr. Garzon, it is purely a matter of therapeutic philosophy or theory. There are two main types of internal healtharian therapy."

Then he continued pompously, "The homeopathic and the allopathic approaches simply represent rival theories about healing.

"Homeopathy is a complete system which aims to trigger off the body's own defenses against sickness by starting up the immune system to fight the illness as cousin Felix said. It does so by means of remedies based on the ancient Hippocratic principle that like destroys like as in two negatives equal one plus. The principle is similar to inoculation which aims to prevent the onslaught of an illness. Dilution and repeated shaking, what we call serial agitation, are used to set the level of potency - that is strength. The more diluted the remedy the more potent it is.

"Such practitioners are known as homeopaths or homeopathic physicians. Allopathic medicine is, of course, orthodox and sets out to oppose the symptoms of sickness with strong drugs which attack those symptoms directly, as Dr. Conn has reminded us so wittily. It's really not all that difficult, Dr. Garzon."

I have never known such arrogance as that with which Plumet pontificated so stiltedly while adding very little to the conversation.

"But by what mechanism and how exactly does this principle work," I asked in a well judged effort to floor him.

Plumet sank into a sulky silence,

obviously not having any original ideas but merely repeating in new phraseology what others had said and written.

Felix O'Neill astonishingly explained, "In inoculation as in vaccination, small weak doses of a disease are given to a healthy patient to build up the immune system so that the system is ready to fight off any later onslaught of the sickness.

"This of course, my dear Garzon, is to enable the patient's system to develop the right antibodies. Homeopathy, which goes back to Hippocrates in the 5th Century B.C. in the Eastern Mediterranean, uses exactly the same practice of like fighting like but after the disease has attacked the body."

"But why is the diluted remedy more powerful than the undiluted?" I asked with genuine interest.

Plumet began to take an extraordinary interest in a piece of carrot and pretended not to hear me.

"Simple," replied the brilliant O'Neill, "as diluted electric particles get smaller they penetrate into the immune cells more deeply. These cells are mainly located in the gastrointestinal system and the small pieces of the reduced size electromagnetic units go deeper into the body's cells."

"Like pointed arrows," cried little

Cormac.

"Out of the mouth of babes and err young persons," added Dr. Conn.

I was stunned by the child's precocity and brightness. It was clear to me that the O'Neill clan were all as sharp as pointed daggers.

O'Neill summed up with a distant abstract glance, "So the patient is given small, diluted, shaken-up doses of the disease as a cure rather than as a preventative."

"But surely this is very dangerous?" I said. "It could make the patient worse."

"Yes," continued Felix O'Neill, "it might indeed make the patient a little worse in some rare cases. Then the treatment is stopped and another remedy is tried. Remember only very watered-down doses are ever given and, in general, homeopathy does work.

"No heavy antagonistic drugs are given with the principle or like fighting like. Yes, there are dangers in all treatments. Some strong drugs can also have real bad side effects in regular allopathic medicine.

"It is important to remember that homeopathy is based on physics and not chemistry. Electromagnetics is the essence of the cures and not chemistry, as is the case with orthodox healthics.

"The remedies of homeopathy are so grossly diluted that they contain no chemical strength whatsoever. Yet their serial agitation has the effect of retaining so much electromagnetic power that the cures work on the level of physics as opposed to chemistry. A healthics that is chemically weak can be electromagnetically strong."

I was absolutely amazed at O'Neill's knowledge of a subject about which I had been somewhat unsure.

Lamely I pointed out to the others that I had been told that homeopathy was merely psychosomatic, working on peoples' minds to make them think that they were cured. I was mortified to hear almost everyone, except the governess and the young girl Doreen, make such cognizant contributions to the allopathic versus homeopathic theories.

I realized that my own contribution had been as dull as dishwater and I could see a glint of satisfaction in the eye of Plumet, who clearly disliked me. For me this was the last straw and I was about to put Plumet on the defensive again with some difficult question when, sensing my self-disappointment, the sensitive Dr. Conn came again to my assistance.

Dr. Conn somewhat reflectively said, "Don't be offended Dr. Garzon by my attack on allopathic surgery, medicine and drugs. Actually it's not all bad. If a man has a broken leg he needs it set, if a woman has a gangrenous arm she needs to get it amputated. If you have an isolated cancer you need to remove it with a knife.

"Herbs or massage or flashing colors or Turkish baths or needle piercing or even homeopathic remedies will just not do the job. While such gentle remedies were working slowly the patient would surely die. On the other hand, the aches and pains of middle-age or an internal upset might well be eased by one or another of these milder long-term oriental remedies.

"I hope that I have not overstated the case against allopathic cures, my dear Dr. Garzon. It is an excellent system in many ways, just not in all ways, and your preventive and unorthodox methods as well as my oriental cures are even being used by doctors in the Imperial Forces. It's a proud tradition that you may one day follow."

"Thank you Dr. Conn," I replied then gulped gratefully.

"No offence then, dear chap?"

I was to take a long time to figure out how he had more or less foreseen that I was considering becoming a consultant on healthics to the navy. It was easy, I had little money at present and few contacts. No brilliance. No choice. Yet Dr. Conn had more or less foreseen all this some time before I had worked it out.

"No offence?" Dr. Conn queried.

"Indeed no, sir," I hastened to agree. "As a researcher I will need to look at the oriental aspects as well as many others. Please feel free to converse on any matter of healthics when we meet. I would be most grateful."

Just as he was about to leave, Dr. Conn sneezed loudly to the one side. "Shut up, shut up," he yelped. "You old halfwit. How can you people just sit there and permit this vile obnoxious anti-social behavior? I've just sneezed out a tooth. See there, it must be on the floor somewhere."

"Why don't you all forbid this outrage?" he asked the children who tittered again delightedly and peeked at the floor from behind their hands. There was, of course, no sign of a tooth.

CHAPTER FIVE
After Dinner

Dr. Garzon enters into a philosophical mode and reflects on the importance of both his and Felix O'Neill's careers.

After the dessert had been eaten, Miss Songana took the children away, no doubt in defense of their beauty sleep.

Dr. Conn withdrew into the library where we could hear the dull murmur of his voice as he dictated to his amanuensis.

My old friend and I sat for some time before the fire discussing the many things which had happened to both of us since our last meeting.

At one point O'Neill suddenly asked me, "What do you think of Miss Songana?"

"She was as fine as fivepence," I answered, "all dressed up to the nines."

"Indeed, she certainly has all the right numbers," said O'Neill briefly then abruptly changed the subject to a more general one.

It was not difficult to find a topic of great interest to both of us. We often took up the problems of the world and solved them to our own satisfaction. Then we were utterly incredulous that the world could be so dedicated to failure and so ungrateful, unintelligent, unpractical and unhelpful as to deny the efficacy of our solutions.

It is the firm belief of educated men that of such is the continually inept nature of society and perhaps indeed here they do have a point. Education and research has a clear morality in world affairs that is not shared by many statesmen.

Indeed, in all my many adventures with O'Neill I never knew one that brought to the light of day so many moral and intellectual issues as this one. Qualities that I usually took for granted with respect to O'Neill now called for a fresh and unbiased rethink. For instance, his unique moral integrity, his independence of mind, his incisiveness of research and reasoning far above even that of the most learned scholars.

Now as I reach the pinnacle of my career I hesitate to say the end, I look back. O'Neill and I often used to talk over new inventions and ideas as educated men are wont to do. The very thought of this amazes me somewhat because O'Neill was an original, unique thinker and I was a mere follower and honored retainer.

However, our solutions to the Irish or South African or Rhodesian or Holy Land questions are matters that have no bearing on the present case. This I hasten to assure you esteemed reader is despite all our grand ideas on those intractable subjects.

Our approaches tended to vary, even to the point of lively argument. I have always been one simply for law and order, whereas O'Neill has always had a more subtle outlook favoring poetic justice. Indeed, it was based on these differences that the lifelong partnership of O'Neill and Garzon developed. Partners must complement not rival each other.

I have always known that O'Neill was an idiosyncratic thinker. This was obvious by his intuitively rational analysis of homeopathy. Rather than following the beaten path to honors and wealth and fame, instead he chose to carve out a solitary and original track to practice a new profession, that of consulting detective. He wanted to help create a new science now known as forensics – the science of justice.

Pioneers such as O'Neill, if they do not get eaten by the cannibals, certainly make no more than a comfortable living.

O'Neill for the most part travels by cab, boat, train or bus whereas those of far lesser ability are seen to arrogantly cruise the Queen's highways in their own coaches and four, driven by servants who are themselves stiff-necked and hard-eyed.

O'Neill has always been a man of the people who can relate equally to potentate or pauper, although he himself is neither. Rather, O'Neill is of that scientific middle group to which I myself belong – this being one of the reasons why I so much appreciate his professional excellence.

Anyhow on my first evening at Seaview House O'Neill relaxed for a little while and elaborated on his intention to work on innovations such as his new camera.

After these pleasant thoughts and looking at the dying embers I bid Felix goodnight and took myself to bed. What a day in body and in mind it had been for me. I was asleep before I hit the sheets. Then I slept like a corpse all night so deeply that I was surprised to be awakened the next morning. At first I thought I had been dead but that could not have been true for surprisingly I felt wonderful. Such is life.

CHAPTER SIX

A Piano and Songana

Felix O'Neill tells Garzon about the mysterious murder of one of the O'Neill children to which a tramp had confessed. Garzon becomes further acquainted with the beautiful oriental governess and later discusses music with Felix.

That first morning at Seaview House I breakfasted informally in the large kitchen at the back of the main wing. O'Neill was rather late in joining me for some ham and eggs since he had been up well into the wee hours working on his new camera and enlarger. He yawned and shook his head as though to clear away the morning mists, an act that somehow reminded me of high hills and lakes.

While I sat in the kitchen eating my breakfast I had a chance to observe that the three old servant maids were nervous and edgy. They seemed a little sharp in their conversation with each other while the ancient groom was as shaky as an old weeping willow in wintertime.

Later, as we sat in the sitting-room, O'Neill breathed in deeply of the fresh seaside air coming in through the window.

He asked me with a smile, "And what do you think of our household?"

I answered that I was very much interested in what I had seen of it. "Your uncle," I said, "is quite a character. I like him very much."

"Yes, he has a warm heart behind all his peculiarities. Your coming as a fellow healtharian seems to have cheered him up. He's never been quite himself since little Deirdre's death. She was the youngest of my Uncle Shane's children and came here with the other two, Cormac and Doreen. However, she had a fit or stroke or something in the shrubbery a couple of months ago. Infant death as you well know, Garzon, is hard to explain at times. The coroner had to return an open verdict. In effect a question mark. When they found the child lying dead in the shrubbery here it was a great blow to Uncle Conn."

"It must have been a shock to Miss Songana also," I remarked.

"Yes, Miss Songana was very much disturbed. She had been here only a week or two at the time. She had been over to Bleakley that day to buy something."

"I was very much interested," I said, "in all that you told me about her in your letter. What an incredible background she has.   Surely she must be romanticizing somewhat."

"No, no. It's all true as gospel. Uncle Conn had her thoroughly checked out. Her father was also an oriental healtharian which of course pleased my uncle no end. However, her father was a bit of a heathen fanatic in spite of his Christian wife.   It appears that he got mixed up in a strange underground community as well as in their mutiny against the Empire so that our government came down heavily on him. Of course this is nothing against the lady herself.

"Indeed my dear uncle felt sorry for her and welcomed her broad international heritage for the children's sake as well as her healtharian family background which has made her highly cognizant of oriental remedies."

"So here she is for sure, as large as life and twice as natural, eh?" I added in amazement.

O'Neill nodded, "That's it, old boy."

"You also said something about a child in her charge being murdered during her former position as a governess. What a horrible double shock to her system. What was that all about?"

"Yes Garzon, her first job was over in Sailport where many ships put in from the east and where the locals are much more cosmopolitan than around here. Anyway, after arriving she found a job with a sea merchant's family looking after their four children. Tragically one of the little girls, a five year-old, was smothered by a low-class mendicant who was not nearly as dim as he pretended."

"You don't mean a daft-Jamie type of person?" I asked.

"Worse," replied O'Neill, "a cunning professional halfwit who earns a living by making people feel superior to him."

"Yes O'Neill, quite a common type of wandering beggar," I nodded, "probably a popular chap. The local yokel of choice."

I was anxious to impress O'Neill with my understanding of phenotypes and O'Neill was suitably pleased. He nodded firmly.

"Precisely so, dear fellow. You've hit on a very interesting point."

"Really O'Neill, what's that?" I asked, doing my best to be modest though professional despite my pleasure at O'Neill's approbation.

"Well, it's very strange in a way. Despite his confession to the vile perversion of infanticide, a group of locals including some members of the freemasons and the exclusive Sailport Brethren has been formed to free him, speculating that he was elsewhere at the time of the murder. They seem to suspect that Miss Songana was somehow involved."

"Suspect Miss Songana? Surely not?" I was astonished.

"Well, they fear that possibly the child was killed by shadowy orientals who are clan members or former associates of her father who was a member of the community of Yeti, the Abominable Snowman of the Himalayas."

"My dear O'Neill," I cried, "I am more inclined to be suspicious of the Sailport religious group than of the oriental one. It's very odd that anyone would try to free a self-confessed child killer unless they were involved themselves in the killing and were afraid of word leaking out. Or unless the jailed man knew too much about err something." I spluttered.

"Perhaps, perhaps and perhaps not." O'Neill was terse, enigmatic and non-committal.

Looking out on the lawn at this point I noticed the governess picking primroses with the children.

"I think I'll take a brief stroll, O'Neill, before hitting the books."

O'Neill nodded amiably. "See you at dinner, dear fellow."

I approached Miss Songana before she saw me and I could not help admiring the beautiful litheness of her figure as her bright red flowery dress swirled around and contrasted with the early primroses and yellow green daffodils. There was a feline grace about her every movement such as I never remember having seen in any other woman. Then I recalled O'Neill's words as to the impression she had made upon the secretary and ceased to wonder at it. As she heard my step she stood up and turned her dark strong face towards me.

She and I conversed cheerfully with the children joining in but, as I recall now so many years later, nothing of any serious import was touched on as is usually the case with first polite conversations. In a little while I excused myself casually and went to read some articles but I confess that I failed miserably to come to terms with the text or to cease from foolish daydreaming.

After an uneventful lunch and dinner O'Neill and I once again found ourselves stretched out on armchairs in the after dinner mode around the great fire of the main hall.

I was still fascinated by the mysterious black-eyed beauty from the orient so I asked O'Neill, "What view of religion does she profess? Does she side with her father or her mother? You mentioned the Yeti and a sacred lamp. What on earth is all that, dear chap?"

"It is so little known in this country, Garzon, that I have so far failed to find a detailed description. I am working on it. However, we naturally never pry into her personal beliefs. Between ourselves I don't think that her convictions are very orthodox.

"Her mother must have been a good Christian woman who taught her daughter piano, drawing, French, Portuguese and Spanish so excellently that Miss Songana can tutor in those subjects as well as in the three R's.

"As for her father, I can't say with much detail but obviously he was not a Christian. When the great rivers of east and west come together who knows what strange waterway will emerge?"

"Or what strange creatures will sail in it," I added, thinking of the flitting, shadowy denizens who were dimly becoming a part of the mysterious landscape in this remote

Celtcountry.

As we spoke, we heard the sound of someone playing a piano in the next room. We both paused to listen. At first the player struck a few isolated notes as though uncertain how to proceed. Then came a series of clanging chords and jarring notes until out of the chaos there suddenly swelled a strange barbaric dirge. It was like the low growl of a trumpet or the subtle clash of cymbals. Louder and louder it began to peal forth in a gust of discordant unsettling moodiness. Then the vexatious strains died back into the mournful chords of a sad adagio. Suddenly we heard the sound of the shutting of the piano and the music was at an end.

"She does that every night," my friend O'Neill remarked, "I suppose it is some oriental ritual. It's deeply tormented music. There is no denying the spiritual power of this nocturne but is it a power for good or evil? I've pursued and tried to capture one or other of her recurrent themes on the bagpipes but with no success.

"Music, my dear Garzon, is good or evil in and of itself, irrespective of the words or outward purpose attached to the sounds. Music may have the words of a divine hymn or be a rollicking drinking song. It may wear any other cunning disguise. However, deep down underneath this cloak, this impersonation and far beyond the mere words or arrangement, the music will have its own integrity and identity.

"Good music heals mind and body. Bad music confuses and destroys. It makes madness and sickness. All music is 'make or break' creative or destructive. It has an inherent characteristic of evil or of good which sometimes contrasts with the verbal facade."

"I agree with you, O'Neill. Music is either good or bad and I'm pretty sure about that piano discordance. Doesn't sound like good music to me, old boy."

O'Neill seemed a little dissatisfied with my agreeable remarks.

"Nor to me either, old chap," he concurred a little wearily. "Bye the bye, how is the research going?"

I sighed and shook my head, "Nothing to write home about, O'Neill. I spent the entire afternoon staring at the title page of Healtharian Statistics Vol. I."

"Never mind, dear chap," he replied sympathetically. "Remember, little by little was Rome rebuilt. Just a smidgeon every day is the key to progress and just opening the book is a start. Tomorrow you might even read a line or two."

I smiled as O'Neill rose. He patted my shoulder and bade me goodnight.

After staring at the bright embers and the darkening eyes of the coals for a long time, I too went to my chambers.

On the way there I passed the open door of the library and caught a fleeting glimpse of Miss Songana studying an old manuscript by the light of her supposedly sacred lamp. I did not intrude. Rather, I went upstairs and decided to read Healthics Jurisprudence for a couple of hours.

I imagined that I would see no more of the inhabitants of Seaview that night but I was mistaken. At about ten o'clock Uncle Conn thrust his white-helmeted red face into the room.

"All comfortable?" he asked.

"Excellent, thank you Dr. Conn" I answered.

"That's right. Keep up the good work. You're sure to succeed," he said, in his sympathetic way. "Good night."

"Good night," I answered.

"Good night," said another voice from the passage and looking out I saw the tall figure of the secretary gliding along at the old man's heels like a long dark shadow but he was addressing the Doctor, not me, adding, "If you have finished with me, Dr. Conn, it is a little warm and clammy in here tonight so if it is alright with you, Doctor, I will sleep in the cottage?"

"Certainly, my dear sir," agreed Dr. Conn. "See you at breakfast. Sleep coolly and well."

I went back to my desk and tried to work for another hour. However, for some time before I dropped off to sleep I pondered over the curious and exciting household of which I had become a member.

CHAPTER SEVEN
Of Quackery and Orthodoxy

At night Garzon is troubled by bad dreams as intruders enter into the grounds of the old house. He briefly discusses prohibition with O'Neill and his great-uncle.

In the weeks following I began to have nightmares. This was in sharp contrast to my first night's good sound sleep at Seaview. It seemed natural at first that I had problems sleeping since the days, although mild, were cloudy and dark and dank.

One night in the wee hours I woke up from a particularly scary and mixed-up dream. When I arose and looked out onto the moonlit lawn I clearly saw four cowled and robed monks walk across the lawn. Later I am sure that I saw four large crows lying dead on the grass like footprints. The next morning there was no sign of them and no one had seen them nor had any explanation. My dreams seemed to be drawn from the common psyche of all men.

Later in my travels I was to become familiar with the legend of the abominable snowman with its counterparts in almost every country. This was purported to be a man-beast of the wastelands. It walked and stalked and loped across the snows of that dreamscape where terror lurks not only in the shadows but in the clear, moonlit open spaces.

In later times in the Himalayas I was to recall the dark significance of the four black birds that lay like giant footprints in the white of the night outside my room at Seaview House.

The message was simple - murder was stalking, jumping and hiding among the roofs and doorways, at the windows and thru the walls of that old house.

One evening O'Neill and I stood calmly in the garden listening to the strange music of the governess. I was invaded by a gloomy sense of foreboding and I mentioned it to O'Neill.

He agreed, "You're right, Garzon. Dark days are following the death of the infant Deirdre. Vile passengers must ride in the carriage of such a troubled coachman."

O'Neill and I had several nightmares of turmoil, violence and death. Later events were to prove that O'Neill and I were not manic but merely sensitive and prescient.

Dr. Conn continued to be a cheerful, devoted and fun-loving host. Yet Dr. Conn's sense of humor, although kindly, was sometimes quite shrewd and highly satiric.

On one occasion he remarked to me, "Now that undergraduate students will receive a practicing certificate in healthics they will be referred to, in a purely honorary way, as Doctor whereas you and I who have earned doctorates for the most part get called Mister. It's all just a part of good old-fashioned contempt for higher education, old chap."

"Well, sir," I replied defensively, "I am always careful to give everyone his or her full title."

"Relax," he laughed, "I am only joking. Why, dear boy, I'm not a clinical doctor at all, merely a Ph.D. researcher and I have the cheek to be researching eastern healthics. Indeed, I'm a mere thesis jockey. I suppose I deserve to be Mistered. I really don't mind."

He shook his head humorously, "I'm just commenting on accepted sentiment and orthodox thought."

Nevertheless I noted silently that his secretary called him Doctor several times in practically every discourse.

O'Neill, who was present, remarked, "Unorthodoxy or even heresy is a term that includes many of civilization's most brilliant minds. It is said that Sir Isaac Newton was a secret Unitarian."

O'Neill looked up and studied the ceiling, then continued.

"Furthermore, what is unorthodox in one country is quite acceptable in another. My dear Garzon, what would you think of the idea of electing our kings or queens just like republican presidents? Or for that matter, our other royal dukes and earls to step down and allow a popular vote on their successors? Perhaps we should think about that?"

"Good heavens, O'Neill," I cried, in horror, "How could you suggest such an outrage? The very idea is preposterous."

Then I noticed that both Dr. Conn and Felix O'Neill were both laughing at Felix's little joke and I soon found myself laughing along with them. Not dangerous radicals, in any way, but good men and true. They were merely making the point that one man's meat is another man's poison.

We all laughed.

I have often thought since then that O'Neill himself was a prime example of the truth of this statement that unorthodoxy was sometimes a sign of genius. To O'Neill genius was merely common sense but my own lack of brilliance at this time was becoming obvious to me with some sorrow.

I was struggling to master my research books mostly on very orthodox western healthics. I was hoping to come up with at least one publishable article on oriental cures about which I understood very little at that time. With this in mind, I determined to listen carefully to Dr. Conn and the governess on all matters relating to eastern healthics.

Indeed, at one time when I was struggling with Healtharian Ethics I did ask Dr. Conn what he thought of the complete prohibition of certain drugs on the grounds that it was best to save humanity from their ill effects.

Dr. Conn explained that prohibition would negate freedom of choice and there would surely be a high cost of enforcement. The worst rogues would jump into a black market that would set up a crime wave. Addicts of the banned drugs would rob and murder to raise funds for the dope they could not do without.

I often remembered his words in later years as prohibition became accepted in the American states but not in other English-speaking countries. Despite his humorous self-disparaging remarks, Dr. Conn had one of the best minds in the country and I have always felt privileged to be able to help him as it later transpired.

Dr. Conn was as gentle and concerned for others as he was brilliant in his chosen field. On this occasion his concern was for his nephew, Felix O'Neill.

"No," continued Dr. Conn, "only self-choice will work. For instance, I would not try to force Felix here to give up his bad habit of smoking weeds that are not good for his health. The choice must be his."

Glancing sideways at Felix O'Neill the good old man continued, "Smoke clogs the lungs and heavy weeds confuse the mind. At some future point polluted mind or lungs may fail prematurely."

I acceded by uttering with enthusiasm a "Yes, indeed sir" to Dr. Conn, not wishing to seem too sermonistic to my friend and host. O'Neill merely nodded his earnest agreement which seemed to close the matter. But of course it did not.

CHAPTER EIGHT

Jealousy

Garzon develops a great admiration for the governess, Miss Songana but jealously concludes that Dr. Conn's secretary, Hermonius Plumet, has developed an equally romantic interest.

Taking a pre-breakfast stroll early the next morning I approached the beautiful governess on the lawn.

"Good morning, Miss Songana," I said. "You are an early riser like me."

"Yes," she answered, "I have always been accustomed to rising at daybreak. I cannot sleep in daylight."

"What a strange and wild landscape." I remarked, looking out over the wide stretch of seas and islands. "I am a stranger to this part of the country, like yourself. How do you like it?"

"I do not like it," she said frankly. "In fact I detest it. It is wintry and bleak and wretched. Look at these," holding up her bunch of primroses, "they call these things flowers. They have not even a smell."

Then I suggested, "You have obviously been used to a more genial climate and tropical vegetation, Miss Songana."

"Oh then Mr. O'Neill has been telling you about me," she said with a smile. "Yes, I have been used to something better than this."

We were standing together when a shadow fell between us and looking around I found that Plumet was standing close behind us. He held out his thin white hand to me with a constrained smile.

"You seem to be able to find your way about already," he remarked as he glanced backwards and forwards from my face to that of Miss Songana. "Let me hold your flowers for you, Miss Songana."

"No thank you," the other said coldly. "I have picked enough and am going inside."

She swept past him and across the lawn to the house. Plumet looked after her with a frowning brow.

"You are an expert in healthics, Dr. Garzon?" he said, turning towards me and stamping one of his feet up and down in a jerky, nervous fashion as he spoke.

"Yes, I am."

"Ah yes, we have heard about you researchers of healthics," he cried in a raised voice with a little crackling laugh. "You are dreadful fellows are you not? According to your reputation there is no standing against you. You have power over the ladies, don't you?"

"A healtharian, sir," I answered coldly, "is usually a gentleman."

"Quite so," he said in a changed voice. "Of course I was only joking, my dear fellow. Surely you can take a ribbing. You are an educated person after all."

"Of course," I said, thinking of the old saw about a joke with a jag.

Indeed, I could not help noticing that at breakfast he kept his mesmeric eyes persistently fixed upon me while Miss Songana was speaking and if I chanced to make a remark he would flash a glance towards her as though to read in our faces what our thoughts were about each other. It was clear that he took a more than common interest in the graceful governess and it seemed to me to be equally evident that his feelings were by no means reciprocated.

CHAPTER NINE
Of Ghosts and Memories

The servants see ghostly visitors during the night and O'Neill and Garzon become further acquainted with the governess.

We had an illustration that morning of the simple nature of these primitive Celtcountry folk. It appears that the two housemaids and the cook, who slept together, were alarmed during the night by something which their superstitious minds contorted into an apparition.

After breakfast I was sitting with Dr. Conn who was busy translating an old manuscript with the help of his secretary. Suddenly there was a tap at the door and the two housemaids, Maisie and Sadie appeared. Close at their heels came the cook, Moira, also terrified. All three were lean, boney and shaking in temerity but mutually encouraging and abetting each other. They told their story like three hens pecking in turn at the chickenfeed.

Sadie talked until her breath failed. Then the narrative was taken up first by Maisie and then by the cook who in turn was supplanted by one of the others. Much of what they said was almost unintelligible to me owing to their extraordinary Celtic dialect but I could make out the main thread of their story.

It appears that in the early morning the cook had been awakened by something touching her face. As she awakened, she had seen a shadowy figure standing by her bed. This figure had immediately glided noiselessly from the room.

The housemaids had been awakened by the cook's cry and whined miserably that they had seen the apparition which was muttering, "Where is the lamp?"

Moira the cook then took a deep breath and stated that she had just received word about a dangerous lunatic being on the loose.

"In view of recent policy it must be the Prime Minister," quipped Plumet with his nose in the air.

"Oh yes, he escaped from Rockfast Prison for the Criminally Insane," continued the cook, unaware of the irony. Her last six words were enunciated very slowly in wide-eyed horror.

No one else had heard of any escaped convict but no amount of cross-examination or reasoning could shake them and the three all wound up by giving notice of intention to quit, which was a practical way of showing that they were honestly scared. They seemed considerably indignant at our want of belief and ended by squirming deviously out of the room, leaving Dr. Conn angry, Plumet contemptuous and myself very much amused.

Soon afterwards I tried to spend nearly the whole of my days in my room and got through a considerable amount of work.

One evening O'Neill and I went down to the rabbit-warrens with our guns. As we came back, I discussed with O'Neill the absurd scene with the servants who had seen a ghost but it did not seem to strike him in the same ridiculous light that it had me. He was serious.

"I heard about this. The fact is," he said, "in very old houses like ours, where you have crude and warped timbers, you get curious effects sometimes which predispose the mind to superstition. I have often heard one or two things at night during this visit which might have frightened a nervous man and still more an uneducated servant. So I explained to the servants that I had made the strange noises. It had been only the wail of my bagpipes. This contributed to their peace of mind and I played an old

Celtic lament on the pipes to them and they agreed to stay after hearing the hollow undulation and ghostly skirling. However, I agreed with them that they must have seen an intruder but one in search of spoil and not servants.

"Also I have made a point of coming and going in the middle of the night on a security patrol and this has calmed them down. Of course all this talk about apparitions is mere nonsense but when once the imagination is excited there is no checking it."

"What have you heard then, O'Neill old fellow?" I asked with interest.

"Oh, nothing of any importance," he answered mysteriously.

The governess and the children arrived and O'Neill whispered to me, "Here come the youngsters and Miss Songana. We mustn't talk about these things before her or else we shall have her giving notice too and that would be a loss to the establishment."

Miss Songana sat down on a little stile which stood on the outskirts of the wood surrounding Seaview and the two children were leaning up against her, one on either side, with their hands clasped round her arms and their chubby faces turned up to hers. It was a pretty picture and we both paused to look at it. She had heard our approach however and springing lightly down she came towards us with the two little ones toddling behind her.

"You must aid me with the weight of your authority," she said to Felix O'Neill. "These little rebels are fond of the night air and won't be persuaded to come indoors."

"Don't want to come," said the boy, with decision. "Want to hear the rest of the story."

"You shall hear the rest of the story tomorrow if you are good. Here is Mr. Garzon who is a doctor and he will tell you how bad it is for little boys and girls to be out when the dew falls."

"So you have been hearing a story?" O'Neill said to the children as we moved together.

"Yes and such a good story," the little chap said with enthusiasm. "Uncle Conn tells us stories but this one was about elephants."

"And tigers and gold and the sacred lamp and the book of wisdom," said the little girl.

"Yes and wars and fighting and the priest of death."

"Faith, my dear," said the governess.

"And the scattered tribes that know

each other by signs and the child that was killed in the wood. Miss Dance knows some splendid stories. Why don't you make her tell you some, Cousin Felix?" asked Cormac.

I have no idea why the children always called their tutor Miss Dance.

"Really Miss Songana, you have excited our curiosity," my friend O'Neill said. "You must tell us of these wonders."

"They would seem stupid enough to you," she answered with a laugh. "They are merely a few reminiscences of my early life."

As we strolled along the pathway which led through the wood we met Plumet coming from the opposite direction.

"I was looking for you all," he said, with an ungainly attempt at geniality, "to tell you that it was dinnertime."

"Our watches told us that," said Felix O'Neill, rather ungraciously.

"And you have been all rabbiting together?" the secretary continued, as he stalked along beside us.

"Not all," I answered, "we met Miss Songana and the children on our way back from taking a few potshots in the field."

"Oh, Miss Songana came to meet you as you came back," he said. This quick contortion of my words, together with the sneering way in which he spoke, vexed me so much that I would have made a sharp rejoinder had it not been for the lady's presence.

I happened to turn my eyes towards the governess at that moment and I saw her glance at the speaker with an angry sparkle in her eyes which showed that she shared my indignation.

However, I was stunned that same night when, about ten o'clock, I chanced to look out of the window of my study to see the two of them, Plumet and Miss Songana, walking up and down in the moonlight engaged in deep and quiet conversation. I don't know how it was but the sight disturbed me so much that after several fruitless attempts to continue my research I threw my books aside and gave up work for the night.

At about eleven I glanced out again but they were gone and shortly afterwards I heard the shuffling step of Dr. Conn and the firm heavy footfall of the secretary as they ascended the staircase which led to their bedrooms located on the upper floor.

CHAPTER TEN
An Amanuensis of Authority

Garzon learns a lot when he discusses eastern healthics with Uncle Conn.

Dr. Conn O'Neill was the original absentminded professor who knew all about his subject but cared little about his appearance or surroundings. I believe that before I had been three weeks under his roof I knew more of what was going on there than he did or so I thought.

Often he seemed totally oblivious to any negative chills or evil presences just so long as he could immerse himself in his work.

One afternoon Dr. Conn, not for the first time, assured me that his great work would be comprehensive and include many remedies from the Near East, Middle East, Mediterranean, the Holy Land, as well as the Far East, stretching out to India, China and Japan.

The old professor gazed into the distance, speaking as one in a trance. "I am thinking of the Secrets of Eastern Healing as a title."

Plumet quietly suggested, "Perhaps Dr. Conn such a standard work could be called: An Encyclopedia of Oriental Healthics?"

Dr. Conn's eyes lit up, "What a wonder of literature such a standard work will be," he cried. "Fasting; Foods and Tonics; Herb and Tree Cures; Handhealings; Needle Piercings. All of these would be major subsections. Plumet make a note of those topics."

Plumet wrote down the chapter titles with the air of one being surprised with long sought birthday presents. His crawling and cringing and grinning smug approbation reminded me of a pet poodle hanging out its tongue to please its owner.

"Oh what a good dog I will be," the dog whines.

"Are you familiar with those concepts which I just listed, Garzon?" asked Dr. Conn.

"Not wholly, sir," I replied evasively.

Dr. Conn was delighted to seize the chance to enlighten me.

"Needle piercing is a form of oriental surgery where sharp pins are driven into the body in certain strategic places so as to direct the body's natural flow of energy or chi. Positive and correct balance of the spine and torso also coordinate limbs and energy flow.

"Hmm, that sounds good but it's perhaps a little disjointed. Plumet, please remind me to divide these concepts into acupuncture and yoga."

"Certainly Dr. Conn. Indeed I will copy both ideas into their respective chapters, subject to your later revision, of course."

"Thank you, Plumet. I don't know how I could get through this monumental work of reference without your help," Dr. Conn added in his grateful way.

"But dear, dear, I am too wordy. I am one writer who never ever gets writer's block. My problem is writer's river, too much flow and gurgle. Any writer who gets writer's block should quit trying to write and become a reader instead. Hee, hee. We writers need more readers. God bless the readers. What would be the point of writing at all if we had no readers?"

He gurgled just like the babbling brook he claimed to be. Uncle Conn certainly sent good words flowing like clear water over the rocks and pebbles of the real seaside where 'come' gives way to 'go'. Indeed, where there is coming and going forever under the moon.

Plumet applauded with several self-satisfied nods of his long head.

As for the younger O'Neill, Felix was almost as dedicated as his uncle. My astute friend Felix spent his days among his test tubes and solutions, ardently devoted to the inventive pursuit of a new camera so accurate that it would be capable of copying written or printed documents. Indeed, in some ways O'Neill was still an auditor at heart, ever following the paper trail intensively and its well trodden road to criminality.

O'Neill seemed happy to have a friend or a congenial companion at hand to whom he could communicate his ideas and scientific results. I was happy to be that friend.

Yet he was ever willing to set aside his own work and to painstakingly encourage me with my research. He always had a penchant for the study and analysis of human character and I in turn found much that was interesting in the microcosm in which I lived. Indeed, I sometimes became so absorbed in my observations that I fear my own research occasionally suffered to a considerable extent.

I was fascinated by the obviously magnetic Plumet. It has been said that the hand that holds the pen wields the power. Indeed, I discovered beyond all doubt that the real master of Seaview was not Dr. Conn but his amanuensis.

My healtharian instinct told me that the absorbing love of oriental remedies, which had been nothing more than a harmless circumthesis in the old man's younger days, had now become a complete monomania which filled his mind to the exclusion of almost every other subject.

Plumet, by humoring his employer upon this area of research until he had made himself indispensable to the old man, had succeeded in gaining complete power over him in everything else. Plumet had not only become the old man's heir to the estate but he managed all the money matters and the affairs of the house, unquestioned and uncontrolled.

However, he had sense enough to exert his authority so lightly that it galled no one's throat and therefore excited no opposition.

I have already expressed my conviction that although Plumet had some tender feeling for the governess, she by no means favored his addresses. But after a few days I came to think that there existed, besides this unrequited affection, some other link which bound the pair together. I had seen him more than once assume an air towards her which can only be described as one of authority. Also, two or three times I had observed them sitting in a corner of the lawn and conversing earnestly into the late hours of the night. I could not even guess what mutual understanding existed between them.

The mystery had deeply disturbed my sense of curiosity.

CHAPTER ELEVEN
A Lovely Lady

Garzon and O'Neill find their curiosity aroused by the mysterious Miss Songana.

It is proverbially easy to fall in love in a country house and my nature has ever been a sentimental one so that my judgment was perhaps a little warped by a tender feeling towards Miss Songana.

In contrast to this O'Neill had set himself, as I later learned, to study her as an economist might read through a series of statistics critically and without bias to look for a trend or an explanation.

With this objective O'Neill used to arrange his life in such a way as to be free at some of the times when Miss Songana took the children out for exercise. In this way O'Neill and the governess had a few conversive walks together and so he gained a clearer and deeper insight into her character. I also followed his lead and did likewise, escorting the dear lady on several walks.

As O'Neill later related to me, Miss Songana was very well read and had an indepth acquaintance with several oriental languages as well as English, French, Spanish and Portuguese, the four great languages of empire. She also had a great natural talent for music.

However, underneath this veneer of culture there was a slash, a knife-cut of the savage in her nature. In the course of her conversation she would, every now and then, drop some remark which would almost startle one by its primitive reasoning and by its disregard for the conventionalities of civilization. However, we could hardly wonder at this when we reflected that she had been a grown woman before she left the wild tribe which her father dominated as a priest and healer.

I remember one instance which struck me as particularly characteristic in which her untutored, original habits suddenly asserted themselves.

On this occasion when O'Neill was not with us, Miss Songana, the children and I were walking along the country road. She was talking of Sailport where she had spent some months when she suddenly stopped short and laid her finger upon her lips.

"Lend me your stick," she said, in a whisper.

I handed the stick to her. Then all at once, to my astonishment, she darted lightly and noiselessly through a gap in the hedge and, bending her lithe body, crept swiftly along under the shelter of a little knoll. I was still looking after her in amazement when a rabbit rose suddenly in front of her and scuttled away. She hurled the stick after the creature and struck it but it made good its escape. However, it was trailing one shattered leg behind it.

She ran back to us exultant and panting. "I saw it move among the grass," she said. "I hit it."

"Yes, you hit it. You broke its leg," I said, somewhat coldly.

"You hurt it," the little boy Cormac cried ruefully in his habit of coming straight to the point.

Suddenly she affected a change in her whole manner. "Poor little beast. I'm sorry I harmed it," she exclaimed.

She spoke little during the remainder of our walk and seemed to all appearances completely cast down by the incident. It was clear to me that the impulsive lady was quite susceptible to suggestion.

For my own part I could not blame her much. O'Neill and I often shot rabbits. The incident was evidently an outbreak of an old predatory instinct based on hunger, though with a somewhat incongruous effect in the case of a fashionably dressed lady on a Celtcountry high road.

Some little time later O'Neill asked me to peep into Miss Songana's private sitting-room while he was out in the garden talking to her.

I did so; she had a thousand little eastern knickknacks in her room which showed that she had come well-laden from her native land. Her oriental remedies of colors had exhibited itself in an amusing fashion. She had gone down to the local market town and bought numerous sheets of pink and blue paper and these she had pinned in patches over the somber covering which had lined the walls before. She had some varicolored tinsel too which she had carefully put up as color therapy in the most conspicuous places.

The whole effect was ludicrously tawdry and glaring and yet there seemed to me to be a touch of pathos in this attempt to reproduce the color therapy of the tropics in an old gray-stone Celtcountry dwelling-house.

Miss Songana was also dedicated to study and intensive readings. At times her book of wisdom, in a strange language, lay under a lamp that she sometimes referred to as the sacred lamp. Her intensive, indeed obsessive, example encouraged me to try to write up my articles on healthics.

CHAPTER TWELVE
A Strange Relationship

Miss Songana seems to have developed an ambiguous feeling for Plumet.

During the first few days of my visit to Seaview the curious relationship which existed between Miss Songana and the secretary had simply excited my curiosity. But as the weeks passed and I became more interested in the beautiful lady, a deeper and more personal fascination had taken possession of me.

I puzzled my brain as to what tie could exist between them. Why was it that while she showed every symptom of being averse to his company during the day that she would walk about with him long after nightfall?

Could it be that the distaste which she showed for him before the others was a blind to conceal her real feelings? Such a supposition seemed to involve a grave depth of dissimulation in her nature which appeared to be incompatible with her façade of civilized frankness. And yet, what other hypothesis could account for the soporific, even hypnotic, power which Plumet most certainly exercised over the governess?

This power showed itself in many ways but was exerted so quietly and silently that none but a close observer could have known that it existed. I have seen him glance at her with a look that was both commanding and menacing. However, the next moment I could hardly believe that his white impassive face could be capable of so intense an expression. When he looked at her in this manner she would wince and quiver as though she had been in physical pain.

Decidedly, I thought, it is some strange feeling and not love which produces such effects.

I was so interested in this question that one morning I spoke to O'Neill about it. He was in his little laboratory at the time and was deeply immersed in a series of chemicals and printing manipulations and distillations which ended in the production of an evil-smelling gas which set us both coughing and choking. I took advantage of our enforced retreat into the fresh air to question him upon one or two points on which I wanted information.

I informed O'Neill that decidedly there was some secret relationship between the governess and the translator.

"Perhaps a common interest in eastern languages?" O'Neill suggested blandly.

I snorted, "I doubt it."

"Try bromide of potassium," suggested O'Neill. "It's very soothing in 20 gram doses. Kills romance in a day."

"How long did you say that Miss Songana had been with your uncle?" I asked.

O'Neill looked at me slyly and shook his finger at me in a negative gesture.

"Looks like you have a problem with onychopathy, old chap. Touch of felon in the finger there, perhaps." I remarked with mock concern.

O'Neill did not answer directly but quickly put his hands in his pockets.

"You seem to be wonderfully interested in the daughter of an obscure eastern rebel," he said shrewdly.

"Who could help it?" I answered frankly. "I think she is one of the most intriguing characters I have ever met."

"Take care of the research, my boy," O'Neill said paternally. "This sort of thing will not help your final article rewrites."

"Don't be ridiculous," I remonstrated. "Anyone would think that I was in love with Miss Songana to hear the way you tell it. I look on her as an interesting psychological problem, nothing more."

"Quite so, an interesting psychological problem and nothing more," replied O'Neill. "I understand perfectly, old boy."

O'Neill seemed to have some of the vapors of the developing liquid still hanging about his system for his manner was decidedly irritating.

"To revert to my original question," I asked, "how long has she been here?"

"About 17 weeks."

"And Plumet?"

"Over two years."

"Do you imagine that they could have known each other before?"

"Ask discretely about that if you wish," replied O'Neill. "But I fear they will tell you nothing. Keep me informed, Garzon. But in fact I doubt if they knew each other before they came to Seaview. I saw the letter of reference in which her former employer in Sailport had traced her early life. She had come from the Orient and had taken employment with the old merchant in Sailport.

"However, recently Plumet has been here continuously in Seaview after his two years on a church scholarship at Mission College. While struggling through eastern languages he had to leave the school without ever graduating and furthermore he appears to have left under a cloud."

"What sort of a cloud, O'Neill?"

"I don't know exactly, Garzon," O'Neill answered pensively. "They have kept it very quiet. I fancy Uncle Conn knows or at least suspects something. But he is very fond of taking up rapscallions and giving them what he calls a second chance, a new start in life based on their professional merit of course, not on mere charity.

"It's good that my uncle is so meritocratic but some of them will give him a start one of these fine days. Plumet says he left college voluntarily to help create the world's greatest encyclopedia of eastern healing. A cock and bull story designed only to flatter Uncle Conn and deflect awkward questions. Of course Plumet helps my uncle with difficult translations as does Miss Songana."

"And so it appears that Plumet and Miss Songana have been absolute strangers until the last few weeks?" I reiterated thoughtfully.

"Quite so; I think we can go back and try out the new camera now. All right, Garzon?"

"Never mind the camera," I cried, detaining him. "There's more I want to talk to you about, O'Neill. If these two have known each other only for a few months, an irrational, odd relationship between them has developed very quickly."

"Yes, I have noticed," replied O'Neill calmly. "I am giving much thought to all the shadowy events of this place but I confess that I have not yet found an explanation. Rest assured that I am trying and that my new invention will be helpful in the investigation," he added cryptically.

I decided to take the bull by the horns.

"O'Neill," I said, boldly, "I have come to the conclusion that Plumet is no more than a bully, a cad and a bounder. I am quite convinced that he is a bad influence on Miss Songana and your uncle and the children. Plumet is purely self-seeking, mercenary or worse. Why, you tell me that he has never even finished his studies."

"Nor have I, Garzon," O'Neill nodded sympathetically and replied quietly, "but it is my Uncle Conn who must be satisfied with Plumet, not you or I, Garzon. It's the old boy's money, not ours."

"True, O'Neill," I shook my head, "but how can a man so lacking in talent be so ingratiating. He's not truly intelligent just merely fieldwise like a wolf or streetwise like a stray cat. Heavens, Dr. Conn could afford to hire a graduate or even a Ph.D. like himself."

"That's true, my dear chap," admitted O'Neill, "but let's wait for proof or at least some evidence before we trouble my uncle."

"But by then it may be too late," I urged.

"Perhaps," agreed O'Neill, "but let's not be too hard on the secretary. You should know by now that the world is full of Plumets. Sycophancy goes further than sagacity. When the meritorious is pushed aside, the meretricious takes over and uncle is a convinced meritocrat who judges on results."

I nodded unhappily, "Still, Plumet is a slithery snake."

"There are many like him in this our Empire, my dear Garzon, who have gone far on very little."

CHAPTER THIRTEEN
Miss Songana and the Secretary

Subtly Garzon tries to warn Miss Songana about Plumet. The household pay a visit to church while O'Neill does some checking on Miss Songana.

I had to admit that O'Neill's indifferent, indeed rather sanguine attitude towards Plumet left me a little uncomfortable. I was no less inclined to worry about Plumet's excessive influence over the governess, the children and the good doctor. However, I was determined to find more ammunition against Plumet as I had a strong hunch that his presence was not for the general weal.

Was his sinister presence connected with the dark shadows on the lawn at night or the visions of strangers in the house or the trembling servants?

I did not know but I was determined to check out the sycophantic secretary as much as possible. I would try again to bring O'Neill to a true sense of the danger regarding the slinking amanuensis.

Considering that Plumet had known Miss Songana for only a short time, I was sure that only some hidden mystery could explain how he had managed to gain his power over her.

After leaving O'Neill I had not gone twenty yards down the gravel walk of the garden before I saw the very couple of whom we had just been speaking. They were some little ways off. She leaning against the sundial and he was standing in front of her and speaking earnestly with occasional expansive gesticulations.

His tall, gaunt figure towering above her and the spasmodic motions of his long arms might have been some great bat fluttering over a victim. I remember that that was the simile which arose in my mind at the time. This was heightened perhaps by the suggestion of shrinking and of fear which seemed to me to lie in every curve of Songana's furtive figure.

The little picture was an illustration of the text upon which I had just been preaching to O'Neill. However, before I had time to come to any conclusion, Plumet caught a glimpse of me and turned away. Then he strolled slowly in the opposite direction into the shrubbery with his companion walking by his side while she cut at the flowers with her sunshade as she passed.

I went up to my room after this small episode with the intention of pushing on with my research but do what I would my mind wandered away from my books in order to speculate upon this mystery.

I had learned from O'Neill that Plumet's antecedents were not of the best and yet he had obviously gained enormous power over his genius of an employer. I could understand this fact by observing the infinite pains with which he devoted himself to the old man's obsession and the consummate tact with which he humored and encouraged Dr. Conn's research whims. But how could I account for the equally obvious power that he wielded over the governess?

After lunch I again took up the subject with O'Neill.

"She has no whims to be humored so what is the nature of Plumet's power over her?" I asked O'Neill.

He replied, "Mutual love might account for the tie between them but my instinct as a man of the world and as an observer of human nature tells me fairly conclusively that no such love exists. If not love, it must be fear or greed - a supposition which is favored by all that I have seen."

What then had occurred during these four months to cause this serene, dark-eyed oriental to fear the long-faced secretary with the sharp voice and the witty repartee?

That was the problem which I had set myself to solve with an energy and earnestness which eclipsed my ardor for research and rendered me impervious to the challenges of my forthcoming collection of articles. A notoriously tough project.

I ventured to approach the subject of my curiosity that same afternoon to Miss Songana, whom I found alone in the library. The two little children having gone to spend the day in the nursery of a neighboring squire.

"You must be rather lonely when there are no visitors," I remarked. "This does not seem to be a very lively part of the country."

"I find that children are always good companions," she answered. "Nevertheless I shall miss both Mr. O'Neill and yourself very much when you go."

"I shall be sorry when the time comes," I said. "I never expected to enjoy this visit as much as I have done. Still, you won't be quite companionless when we are gone, you'll always have Mr. Plumet."

"Yes, we shall always have Plumet." She spoke with a bitter intonation.

"He is a pleasant companion," I remarked, "witty, well informed and bright. I don't wonder that old Dr. Conn is so fond of him."

As I spoke in this way I watched my companion intently. There was a slight flush on her dark cheeks and she drummed her fingers impatiently against the arms of the chair. She was obviously disturbed and I found it tactful to change the subject.

Sure enough, on the following Sunday, Plumet again showed an unpleasant streak in his personality. It happened as everyone stood at the great front door waiting for the team and coach to take us to church.

Dr. Conn, devoted as he was to the mysteries of eastern healthics, was still the local squire and a true Christian gentleman although he wore neither his politics nor his religion like a medal of honor as many do who are mere impostors and hirelings.

One Saturday night during my first weeks at Seaview, Dr. Conn had approached me a little gingerly in the library.

"Here, have a seat, old boy. Can I get you a drink?"

"Thank you, sir," I replied gratefully. "It's a nice time of evening to relax."

"Look, Garzon, it's like this. All week long I'm a scholar, as eccentric as they

come. I can afford to do my own thing and
at my age and why not? But on Sunday
mornings I become a country squire, lay
aside my big boots and white sun helmet
and try to set a good example to the village
folk and the servants and children.

"I dress up in my Sunday-best and well
fact is old chap we pretty well all go to the
parish church. I say pretty well because no
one would ever expect Felix to be able to sit
still for more than an hour, ha, ha. There is
no compulsion you understand Garzon but
now that you've been here a couple of weeks
you would be most welcome and it would
look good to the children if you could come."

"Of course, Dr. Conn," I replied. "I was
brought up as a Christian, you know. I
would be honored and delighted to join your
little church party."

"Great, old boy. We meet on the front
porch at 10 o'clock and the coach will take
us. You know Garzon, some good Christians
are not good churchmen and some
churchmen are not good Christians. I make
no claim to be either but our weekly visit to
church is our way of helping to introduce
the children to growing up, being friendly
with neighbors and making common cause
with humanity. As far as I'm concerned
one's real religion is a very private and

personal matter, even Miss Songana agrees with this although she is really from quite a different background of faith."

"What exactly is her faith, Dr. Conn?" I asked naively. He looked around guiltily and lowered his voice.

"I'm afraid that's not quite clear, dear fellow. But," he brightened, "her references are very good and she is a most suitable person to teach the young I am sure."

He broke off and stared into space with a puzzled look, "I really feel quite sure about her and her, ah, ability in eastern languages also."

"I have also been very impressed with the dear lady," I assured the good doctor.

This seemed to please him and we changed the subject but the shadow that had seemed for a moment to pass over the old professor made my mind drift away and a cold shiver passed across my shoulders like a cloak of snow as I contemplated the unexplained death of a child.

Then there was the abject terror of the ancient groom, still scared and trembling, and the three old servant maids always devious and glancing sideways as though afraid of the madness in the shadows. And why not?

Just what was lurking in the shades and toils of this old house? Ghosts, thieves, escaped convicts, fiendhounds, murderers, cryptic books, hidden lairs, midnight friars, druidic celebrants, foreign killers, avengers? Who could tell? But something was not what it seemed.

At any rate, the next morning I had presented myself in my Sunday best at 10 o'clock on the front steps. Miss Songana and the two children were there, all starched up, along with the amanuensis in his dark gray suit and white collar. The three trembling maidservants were there in shawls, long flimsy dresses and white hats. There was no sign of Felix as his uncle had foreseen. Over to the east side of the house the ancient groom was rigging up the team and Dr. Conn was inspecting the coach.

The company were a little stiff and Plumet tried to loosen up the terrified servants by making a few rather silly jokes.

"It's cold," he shivered. "I guess we are the frozen chosen."

He smirked, "Trouble with churches is they're open to all the sinners of the day, so you meet nothing but rogues there."

Only the children giggled though the others smiled politely.

Undeterred he continued, "They say the bigger the Bible you carry the bigger the hypocrite you are.

"You know everyone in church is selling something - trouble is no one wants to buy it - so you're better going to market."

And so on and so on. Finally the coach arrived and we joined Dr. Conn and went on our way.

When the service had finished, I met with Felix on the lawn after we'd had lunch.

"Didn't see you at church, O'Neill. I suppose you were in the back of the balcony," I remarked blandly.

O'Neill smiled, "Last time I went to church the clergyman threw cold water all over me. That's why I never went back," he added cheerfully.

Felix pretended to shiver at the very prospect. He shuddered, "Brr, brr."

Then he lowered his voice, "Just between ourselves, Garzon, I was glad of the chance to check out that book of wisdom while Miss Songana was at church."

"What did you make of it?" I asked.

He shook his head. "Neither head nor tails. I might as well have gone to church for all I learned," he smiled.

"Everybody makes jokes about going to church," I remarked. "It is one of the mainstays of respectable humor but I must say that Plumet's jokes sounded a little strained insofar as he was standing, prayer book and Bible in hand, dressed up in his Sunday best and supposed to be setting a good example to the children. I did rather think that Plumet was a bit flippant about that, O'Neill. Didn't you say he went to Mission College on a church scholarship?"

He nodded, "Fellowship in missionary languages or something of that order. No pun intended."

"Well," I added, "all that sneering and sniping of his sounded a little bit like biting the hand that feeds you. No harm in a joke but there's a proper time and place."

I paused as O'Neill stiffened and gave me a sharp look.

"You have just made a very interesting remark, Garzon. Why could I not see that? I thank you for your insight, old chap."

I was at a loss but pleased, "What insight was that, O'Neill?"

"Biting the hand. Really, I must check that out."

Drawing together the flowing fold of his tweed cape, squaring his shoulders against the keen seaside wind and robinhood hat atop, O'Neill stalked off brooding heavily.

CHAPTER FOURTEEN
Philosophy of a Lady

Hoping to get to know her better, Garzon asks Miss Songana about eastern healthics and philosophy.

After that discussion with my friend O'Neill, I decided to follow his suggestion that I should carry out some investigation myself.

In particular, he specifically asked me to make a real effort to find out more about the mystical book of wisdom. Even O'Neill, the auditor extraordinary, had failed to uncover its secrets and had now concluded that this book called for a less direct, more subtle approach. But what?

After some thought I came up with a simple ploy. I would ask Miss Songana some seemingly innocuous questions. These would be all of a healtharian or general nature. Then I would seek to infer any underlying philosophy and any patterns of opinions or recurring ideas. In this way I might get some sense of any consistent underlying ideology in which O'Neill was particularly interested.

"Try not to arouse her suspicions by sniping at Plumet," pleaded O'Neill.

"Of course not," I retorted indignantly but I'm afraid I did not quite live up to this undertaking.

At any rate, shortly after I agreed on this plan with Felix, I had an opportunity to approach Miss Songana in the library as she pored over the book of wisdom lit by the sacred lamp as she called it. I seated myself near her and then remarked that I had been looking up some oriental healtharian practices but had not yet been able to find any overall eastern philosophy of healing.

Miss Songana glanced up reflectively and thought for a moment.

"No, there is no one system that covers all of eastern healing," she agreed. "There are several different main languages and philosophical groups but as for my own observations I have found a pattern of healing that is based on a five-fold methodology."

"Please go on, Miss Songana," I begged her. "I need to know these things to assist me with my post-doctoral research."

"Well," she continued. "The five basic methods are applied through the physical senses which lead into the mind. You are no doubt aware of these, Dr. Garzon?"

"Of course, Miss Songana," I replied, "But I am less cognizant than you may be of the actual methods so perhaps you could explain."

Miss Songana considered thoughtfully.

"This no doubt is the best healing method of all," she said. "In my opinion it is sensory healing through the major senses of eyesight, smell, taste, hearing and touching. This pattern is really quite holistic. Indeed, I could say that it is the only truly comprehensive approach to healing and remaining in good health."

I was enthralled with her insights, her orderly mind and her understanding of physiatrics. This was equaled by her extreme attractiveness.

"Well," she continued, "such healings could be, for instance, pressure on parts of the hands or feet which are said to correspond to and rejuvenate various organs. Again, massage is pressure applied by hand to aid circulation and to relieve tension and stress."

I was astonished and fascinated as I nodded encouragement to the lady.

"Massage helps to heal injuries faster, improves breathing and muscle movement. Shiatsu or tuina is pressing hard on various energy points to free the body's vital energy or chi. That would be one way of relieving digestive problems, some headaches such as migraines even insomnia, high blood pressure or rogue lymphatic flow."

"You're getting me into deep water there," I informed Miss Songana, sadly. "I'm afraid I know little about these eastern remedies despite my former studies. I've no idea how those therapies work."

"Well," she replied in a kindly tone, "oils such as almond, sesame, mustard, olive, coconut or from other herbs or plants are massaged into the head as the scalp is moved to and fro, back and forth. The oil is rubbed into the skin of the scalp, neck and upper spine. Hot and cold stones are then pressed into crucial energy points of the body. Tai Na is Chinese massage. Shiatsu is acupressure that is Japanese massage. Acupuncture is puncturing with pins into specific points in the body to secure healing by activating the body's own defense and immunities.

"You will be familiar with internal healthics through the mouth or invasively through the skin by way of knives or pins. But there is also therapy on the surface of the body such as water treatment or deep manipulation beneath the surface such as by bone or spine setting.

"Then there are healing colors and lights which are absorbed by the eyes; music which enters through the ears; flowers and fresh air which bring healing by way of smell; hand healing or hot baths apply pressure to the skin, herbal and food remedies are eaten or drunk through the mouth, often along with clear water.

"These are just some of the main techniques that are applied by way of the eyes, nose, mouth, ears and skin.

"Gentle exercise and its deep breathing draws all these five sensory cures together. It coordinates energy flow to the mind which acts as the ultimate receptor of all these healings. The mind in turn communicates through prayer with the great healing powers of the universe so that healing is received into and channeled throughout the entire body."

"I don't quite understand?" I asked.

"It is quite simple," she smiled. "The mind is believed, all over the Orient, to be the link between gods and humans. Short-term fasting sharpens the senses and prayer puts the sick one in touch with the great powers of good in the universe."

"And what of the powers of evil?" I asked. "Do they not attack us to wreck our health?"

She glanced down with a look of slight embarrassment and stumbled her words.

"Well, powers of evil must be and need always to be dealt with. By the way, it is getting a little late. Shall we resume this conversation at some other time?"

I thanked her for her insights and remarked that she was clearly benefiting from the book of wisdom.

"Yes, enlightenment is by the rays of the sacred lamp," she replied mysteriously.

"Both of those artifacts, book and lamp, must be very valuable or you would not hide them at night," I remarked.

She nodded evasively but seemed relieved that I did not pursue the subject of moral rights or wrongs. I chastised myself that her religious beliefs were none of my business.

Thanking her politely for her thought-raising explanations, I said sincerely, "Now I realize why Dr. Conn is so enthralled with your help in his research as well as your devotion to the children."

She placed her hands together and bowed pleasantly and I thought happily as I withdrew.

CHAPTER FIFTEEN

Kill Plumet

Garzon tries again to probe the strange ambiguity of the relationship between the governess and the amanuensis.

Shortly after my recent conversation with Miss Songana, I tried again to sound her out about Plumet.

"His manner may be a little cold at times," I suggested, "although he has been a great help to Dr. Conn."

But she interrupted me, turning on me furiously with an angry glare in her dark eyes.

"Why do you always want to talk to me about him?" she asked.

"I beg your pardon ma'am," I replied submissively, "I did not know that it was a forbidden subject."

"I do not wish ever to hear his name," she cried, passionately. "I hate it and I hate him. Oh, if I only had someone who would admire me, that is, as men admire ladies away over the seas in my own land. I know what I would say to such an admirer."

"What would you say to him?" I asked, astonished at this extraordinary outburst.

She leaned forward until I seemed to feel the quick pants of her warm breath upon my face.

"Kill Plumet," she said. "That is what I would say to such a suitor. Kill Plumet and then you can come and talk of your admiration for me."

Nothing can describe the intensity of fierceness with which she hissed out these words from between her white teeth.

She looked so venomous as she spoke that I involuntarily shrank back from her.

Could this pythoness be the demure lady who sat every day so primly and quietly at the table of Dr. Conn?

Could this be the lady governess who taught the orphaned little O'Neill cousins to speak Mandarin along with other civilized accomplishments?

Certainly I had hoped to gain some insight into the mystery by my leading questions but I had never expected to conjure up such a spirit as this. She must have seen the horror and surprise which was depicted on my face, for suddenly her manner changed and she started to laugh nervously.

"You must really think me mad," she said. "You see it is the eastern culture breaking out again. We do nothing by halves over there, either devotion or hating."

"And why is it that you hate Mr. Plumet?" I asked.

"Ah, well," she answered in a subdued voice, "perhaps hate is rather too strong a word after all. Dislike would be a better term. There are some people against whom you cannot help having an antipathy even though you are unable to give an exact reason."

It was evident that she regretted her recent outburst and was endeavoring to explain it away by toning it down.

"Tell me what is in the book of wisdom. I am devoted to such tomes," I asked.

"It's just a lesson in eastern lore," she answered vaguely with a sulky downward glance.

As I saw that she wished to change the topic of conversation, I helped her to do so. I made some remark about an illustrated book of oriental village elders, characters, leaders, rajahs and the like which she had taken down before I came in and which still lay upon her lap. Uncle Conn's collection was an extensive one and was particularly rich in English language work of this class.

"This is good and is very true to life indeed," she continued picking out a picture of an oriental priest with a picturesque headdress upon his head.

"My father was dressed like that when he rode out on his white horse and inspired all the warriors to do battle with the enemy. My father was chosen out from amongst them all, for they knew that he was a great priest and inspired leader as well as a great healer.   The people would be led by none but a tested and tried priest with real spiritual powers on his side.   He is dead now as are all those who followed his priesthood.   There are none who are not scattered or slain whilst I, his daughter, am a servant in a far land."

"No doubt you will go back to the East some day," I said, in a somewhat feeble attempt at consolation.

She turned the pages over listlessly for a few moments without answering.   Then she gave a sudden little cry of pain as she paused at one of the prints.

"Look at this here," she cried, fearfully. "It is one of our healer-wanderers. He is a guru.   This picture is very like someone I thought I saw in a dream."

Her voice wavered. The picture which attracted her was one which represented a particularly uninviting-looking traveler with what looked like a miniature lamp in one hand and a strange book in the other.

"The book that he holds is his secret guide," she said. "Of course, he wouldn't go about with it openly like that nor would he bear the lamp at all times. Still, the picture is symbolic and he is as he should be.

"Many a time have I been with such a guru upon the moonless nights when the adherents of Yeti the man-beast were prowling on ahead through the jungle. The heedless stranger heard the night cries far away carried by the hot, humid air and knew not what it might mean. Ah, that was a life that was really worth the living."

"Really?" I wondered. "And what may a secret guiding book be and the guru and the lamp and all the rest of it?" I asked.

"Oh, they are terms that have special religious meanings," she answered, with a far gaze. "You would not understand them."

I said, "This picture is marked as Fakir and I always thought that a Fakir was a beggar."

"That is because you know no better," she observed, "of course Fakirs are beggars but they call many people beggars who are not really so. A Fakir is far, far more than a mere beggar. This picture of a man sitting cross-legged is a holy man and most likely a guru, a spiritual adviser as well as a healer."

I pointed to some of the pictures in the book and noted that oriental healers often cross legs when sitting.

"But surely this blocks the veins and slows blood flow," I added.

"Possibly it slows down the blood to a slight extent but cross-legged exercises promote the flow of energy throughout the body with healing and regenerative effect," replied Miss Songana.

I was dumbfounded. I had never even heard of flow of energy until Dr. Conn had recently mentioned it in passing. Now Miss Songana referred to it as though it were a healtharian basic. My first thought was that I certainly did not know as much as I thought I did about the topic.

However this, I was to find out, was much easier said than done. The stylish radiance of Miss Songana, as well as the threats and enigmas of Seaview, had the effect at times of stultifying my brain. This put my brain into a state of shock in which I could not easily concentrate on anything except the dreams and dangers of the reclusive estate.

Nevertheless, I reported to O'Neill all of Miss Songana's opinions and ideas just as he and I had agreed.

When I recounted Miss Songana's 'Kill Plumet' outburst to O'Neill he appeared to be quite mystified, shook his head and replied, "Perhaps you were not as tactful as you might have been."

"Perhaps so," I conceded ruefully.

O'Neill seemed puzzled and upset by my report and his response was to be a real shock to me. Incredibly, his reaction was to stare into space and declare that he might need to leave sometime in the near future for the Capital.

CHAPTER SIXTEEN
O'Neill Leaves

Felix O'Neill takes a trip to the Capital as he senses mystery, even danger brooding in the air at Seaview.

Over the next few days I met with Miss Songana on a frequent basis in the hope that she might give me more understanding of oriental cures and remedies. For this was a subject about which she loved to talk.

One day we discussed remedies in the drawing room. Quite suddenly, right before my eyes, I saw a change come over her face. She gazed with a rigid hypnotic stare at the open window close behind me.

I looked around and there peering stealthily at us through the windowpane was the face of the sinister amanuensis. I must confess that I was startled at the sight. For with its corpselike pallor the dolichocephalic head might have been one which had been severed from its shoulders. When he saw that he was observed, he reached inside and threw open the sash.

"I'm sorry to interrupt you," he said, looking about with a hypocritical air of innocence, "but don't you think Miss

Songana that it is a pity to be boxed up in a closed room on such a fine day? Won't you come out and take a stroll in the sunny spring air?"

Though his words were courteous they were uttered in a harsh and almost menacing voice so as to sound more like a command than a request. The governess rose and without protest or remark glided away to put on her bonnet. This was another example of Plumet's magnetic authority over her.

As he looked in at me through the open window, a mocking smile played about his thin lips as though he would like to have taunted me with this display of his power. With the sun shining in behind him he might have been a demon in a halo. He stood in this manner for a few moments gazing in at me with concentrated malice upon his face. Then I heard his heavy footfall scrunching along the gravel path as he walked around in the direction of the door to join the erudite governess in the exquisite sharp air of a seaside walk.

For some weeks after the discussion in which Miss Songana confessed her hatred of the secretary, things ran smoothly at Seaview. I was able to have several such long conversations with her as we rambled about the woods and fields with the two little children. However, I was never able to bring her around to the subject of her outburst in the library, nor did she tell me anything which threw any light at all upon the problem which interested me so deeply.

It became clear that there was a real mystery concerning the background of both Plumet and Songana or perhaps Dr. Conn himself. I needed to find out more from the governess concerning her fear of Plumet.

Whenever I made any remark which might lead in that direction she either answered me in a guarded manner or else discovered suddenly that it was high time that the children were back in their nursery.

The result was that I came to despair of ever learning anything from her lips. Perhaps my questioning of her, though I tried to be tactful, had given her the impression that she was under investigation or observation as indeed she was.

During this time I worked on my research spasmodically and irregularly. Occasionally the learned Dr. Conn would shuffle into my room with a roll of manuscripts in his hand and would read me extracts from his research. Whenever I felt in need of company I used to go a-visiting to O'Neill's laboratory and he in turn would normally come to my chambers fairly regularly. Sometimes I used to vary the monotony of my readings by taking my books out into an arbor in the shrubbery and working there during the day.

As to Plumet, I avoided him as much as possible and he, for his part, appeared to be by no means anxious to cultivate my acquaintance any further.

So the spring days blew along briskly towards summer.

One day, with only a few weeks to finish my articles, O'Neill came to me with a telegram in his hand and a look of considerable perplexity upon his face. "I must go up to the Capital to check out this mystery."

In view of his previous reaction to my report on Miss Songana, this intention was naturally not unexpected.

"I suppose you won't be gone long?" I said.

"A week or two perhaps. It's rather unfortunate just when I was in a fair way towards finding answers. I was hoping to solve the mystery here but alas I cannot, especially after the information you gave me about Miss Songana's repressed homicidal wishes for Plumet and who knows, perhaps for others? No. I must dig deeper."

O'Neill closed his eyes, raised his head and gazed sightlessly into the distance.

Again O'Neill brought to mind the image of a hard-trekking pilgrim pursuing his spiritual mountains.

"You'll find the mystery here when you come back," I said, laughing. "There's no one here who is likely to solve it in your absence."

"What bothers me most is leaving you here," he continued. "It seems such an inhospitable thing to ask a fellow down to a lonely place like this and then to run away and leave him."

"Don't mind about me," I answered. "I have too much to do to be lonely. Besides, I have found attractions in this place which I never expected. I don't think any few weeks of my life have ever passed more quickly than the last."

"Oh, they have passed quickly have they?" said O'Neill, and smiled quietly to himself. I am convinced that he was still under the delusion that I was hopelessly in love with the governess. I can't understand why after the unvarnished and brutally honest report on her which I had recently given to O'Neill.

Anyhow he went off that day by the early train promising to write and tell us his address in town, for he did not know yet at which hotel he would put up. I little knew what a difference this trifle would make in depriving us of his shrewd scientific mind nor what was to occur before I set eyes upon my friend once more.

At the time, I was by no means grieved at his departure. It brought the four of us who were left, Songana, Plumet, Dr. Conn and myself, into closer observation and seemed to favor the solving of the problem in which I found myself from day to day becoming more immersed as in one of the local mires.

I was indeed sinking into a sudden and unforeseen mire of mysterious ghosts of all those who walked by night in the old house and whose footsteps fell throughout its deadly grounds.

CHAPTER SEVENTEEN
A Friar's Warning

A group of friars from the local monastery visit the O'Neill mansion.

It was a quiet and peaceful early June evening and Felix was away in the Capital. We all sat around garden tables and participated in that most delightful of summer rituals - eating biscuits and sipping tea. The governess and the two children were at one table, I lounged comfortably at another while Plumet and Dr. Conn sat at a third.

It had been a bright and sunny day and now the sun was beginning to become fuzzy as it went down to bed over the misty druidic landscape. At least this was how it seemed and a pleasant illusion it was, as I have always imagined it. No matter where on the face of the earth I have traveled when I watch the sun go down I think of the ancient wanderings of the Gael. They remain the people of the west, of the setting sun of the land of saints and scholars. From there came many of the world's founding fathers so many years ago.

Here in the fierce land of the Celtcountry, home of the bravest seamen, pilgrims and world travelers, I was again daydreaming of the time when I would no longer have to concern myself with intensive research in my chosen field. Would I ever become a true expert in eastern healthics and use my expertise towards doing some good in the world?

As I daydreamed, I could vaguely hear Dr. Conn sneezing and denouncing himself as an old freak to the delight of the children.

In our relaxed mood we had not seen four friars approaching us from the direction of the sunlight until they were almost upon us. In fiery haloes, hands crossed into huge sleeves, cowled and robed in dark gray they were suddenly only a few yards away.

As they continued to approach, a nervous Miss Songana stood up and ushered the children protectively into the house, muttering something about bedtime. She did not seem to hear Dr. Conn call out not to be alarmed and to take it easy. She was clearly frightened and not at all relaxed. Shortly after she entered the house the servants, sensing something strange, began to peer out fearfully from the doorway where they had been waiting to clear the seats, tables and tableware when the sun would go down.

The monks approached and crossed themselves with the sign of the cross then bowed to the company but addressed Dr. Conn.

"Dr. O'Neill. We greet you in the name of the Church. I will come to the point at once so as not to detain you. We are following rumors of heathen ceremonies in this area and ask if you have you seen anything suspicious?"

"Certainly not," replied Dr. Conn.

Likewise Plumet and I shook our heads.

"We would not tolerate such with two young children in residence," added the gentle old scholar.

"Yes," nodded the leading monk, a powerful man with an intense, lined, ruddy face, framed in iron gray hair. His blue eyes pierced us. "Yes indeed, there are two children now but there used to be three. The spirit of one may not be at rest. Her death was never explained."

Dr. Conn was shattered. He swallowed hard but said nothing.

"Can we speak to your servants?" the monks asked.

"Of course," Dr. Conn beckoned to the four lurking servants who crept out fearfully in their usual state of quivering wonderment and tremulation.

The chief friar stepped forward, his back towards us and spoke quietly to the open-mouthed servants. While I could not hear his words, the old groom who was facing us said something that sounded like pagan meetings and shook his head vigorously. I also caught the words, the Grayreaper, as the frail and shaking old maidservants cringed in terror.

"Nay, none Brother," they muttered. Then the servants crossed themselves as though to repudiate the very thought of such a blasphemy.

The leading monk turned back to Dr. Conn. "Dead blackbirds of prey, symbols of evil, to destroy our sprinkling of the blest water of life have been strewn in the wake of our mercy treks. So be watchful and wary sir. And your friends also."

He extended his robed arm towards Plumet and I, then inclined his head didactically towards us.

"May God protect you all." Then the friars bowed.

We respectfully nodded our thanks for the warning but although I was upset the warning came as no great surprise to me. The monks turned and walked away as bizarrely as they had come, into the misty sun still setting on the rough uneven cliffs.

"This is a bad business," muttered Dr. Conn, shaking his head unhappily. "No good can come of this."

"Indeed Doctor, it is worrying," agreed the sycophantic secretary. "So many times it has been proven that there is no smoke without fire. Of course, sir, the fire often burns deep and needs a subtle spiritual insight to discern its meaning."

I glanced at Plumet sharply but could not be sure what he knew or what he was really thinking so bland and inscrutable was his visage.

Yet, although somewhat shocked by the visit of the monks, I wondered if perhaps these dark friars might have been misleading us for some nefarious reasons best known to themselves.

CHAPTER EIGHTEEN
A Country Walk

Garzon, Miss Songana and the O'Neill children visit a nearby fishing village and encounter a strange Indian Fakir.

About a quarter of a mile from the house of Seaview lies the straggling little fishing village of the same name. It consists of some twenty or thirty slate-roofed cottages and an ivy-clad church hard by a famous tavern run by a distinguished Hispanic cook and baker named Senor Juan Gallegos.

In this picturesque setting, shortly after the day on which Felix O'Neill left us, Miss Songana and the two children walked down to the village post office and I volunteered to accompany them.

Plumet would have liked well to prevent the excursion or at least to have gone with us. Fortunately, Dr. Conn was in the throes of translation and it seemed that the services of his amanuensis were indispensable to him.

It was a pleasant walk I remember for the road was well shaded by trees and the birds were singing merrily overhead. We strolled along together and talked of many things while the little boy and girl ran on ahead of us laughing and romping.

Before reaching the post office, one has to pass the pub already mentioned. As we walked down the village street we became conscious that a small group of people had assembled in front of this building.

There were a dozen or so ragged boys and draggle-tailed girls with a few poorly dressed women as well as a couple of loungers from the bar. This was probably as large an assemblage as ever met together in the annals of that quiet neighborhood.

We could not see what it was that was exciting their curiosity but the children scampered on and quickly returned with a brimful of information.

"Oh Miss Dance," Cormac cried, as he dashed up, panting and eager, "there's a black man there like the pictures in the books and the ones you tell us stories about."

"A gypsy, I suppose," I said.

"No, no," said Cormac, with decision, "he is blacker than that isn't he Doreen?"

"Yes Miss Dance, blacker than that," the little girl echoed.

"I suppose we had better go and see this wonderful person," I suggested.

As I spoke I glanced at my companion. To my surprise Miss Songana was very pale and her great dark eyes appeared to be luminous with suppressed trepidation and bewilderment.

"Aren't you well?" I asked.

"I do not know, Dr. Garzon," she whispered, slowing her step. "I'm not sure what is going on. I was not expecting to meet a foreign person here. Yet I did have a premonition, a dream."

It was certainly a curious sight which met our eyes when we joined the little circle of rustics. It reminded me of the picture of the guru in the books of eastern lore in the library at Seaview House.

In the center of the circle of homely Celts there stood a tall oriental wanderer, lithe and graceful, his linen clothes stained with dust and his brown feet projecting through his rude shoes. It was evident that he had traveled far and long.

He had a heavy stick in his hand on which he leaned and his dark eyes looked thoughtfully away into space, apparently careless of the throng around him. His picturesque attire, with his colored Eastern headdress and his swarthy, gray-bearded face had a strange and incongruous effect upon all the prosaic surroundings and laughing children.

"Poor fellow," Miss Songana said to me, speaking in a fearful gasping voice. "He is tired and hungry no doubt and cannot achieve his wants. I will speak to him."

She went up to the Oriental and said a few words in a native dialect and he responded in a form of English spoken with an oriental accent.

While I could not understand him completely, he shouted out something that sounded like, "I seek the sacred lamp and the book of wisdom."

Never shall I forget the effect which those few syllables produced. Without a word, the governess fell straight down upon her face on the dusty road and absolutely groveled at the feet of the strange guru. I had read of eastern forms of abasement when in the presence of a superior but I never imagined that any human being could have expressed such abject humility as was indicated in this dear lady's attitude.

The guru stared at Miss Songana with a fierce hypnotic glare. He spoke again in a sharp and commanding voice, "Rise up dear lady," on which she sprang to her feet and stood with her hands clasped and her eyes cast down like a slave in the presence of her master.

Mine host Juan and the little crowd, who seemed to think that the sudden prostration had been the prelude to some conjuring feat or acrobatic entertainment, looked on amused and expectant. Some locals nudged each other and smirked oafishly.

One yokel remarked jokingly, "He speaks like a Welshman."

Indeed, the dark traveler's melodious accent was similar to the mellifluent English of Wales.

"Would you mind walking on with the children and posting the letters?" the governess pleaded with me. "I should like to have a word with this good man."

I complied with her request and while at the post office I received a telegram from O'Neill which I could not understand at that time, said nothing of it, and when I returned in a few minutes the two Orientals were still conversing. The wiry, muscular oriental appeared to be giving a narrative of his adventures or detailing the causes of his journey, for he spoke rapidly and excitedly with quivering fingers. He was clearly remonstrating and pleading and arguing and demanding a lamp or a book or something to sell perhaps. Miss Songana shook her head and spread her hands in a hopeless gesture.

Thinking that perhaps the mendicant was begging, I offered him some money. He seemed surprised, then laughed loudly and accepted it. He said with gleaming eyes, "I need this. Money is the root of all evil."

I noticed that Juan and the locals, as well as the children, were also guffawing at the foreigner.

Miss Songana listened intently, giving an occasional start or exclamation, which showed how deeply the man's statement had upset her. I found it most difficult to follow the man's broken English.

"I must apologize for detaining you so long in the sun," Miss Songana said, addressing the guru. "I will leave something for you to eat at our gates."

Then turning to me at last, she implored me, "We must go home or we shall be late for dinner."

With a few parting sentences, mainly given to denials and refusals, she left her dusty acquaintance still waving his arms wildly and holding forth volubly as he harangued the air above the village street. We strolled thoughtfully homewards with the children.

CHAPTER NINETEEN

Dead Dreams and Other Shades

Garzon continues to admire the brilliant Miss Songana but realizes that her friendship with Plumet has apparently begun to blossom.

The governess, the two children and I approached the long driveway to Seaview House where the tree branches formed a gnarled roof.

When we were well out of earshot of the mendicant I asked Miss Songana, with natural curiosity, "Well, who is he and what is he? What an odd fellow."

"He comes from the far provinces, near the land of the book of wisdom. He is not one of us. It has been quite a shock for me to meet a foreign speaking co-religionist so unexpectedly. I feel quite upset. We could converse only in English though. This is not uncommon since there are hundreds of oriental tongues."

"It must have been unpleasant for you," I remarked.

"Yes, very unpleasant," she responded uneasily.

"But why did you fall down like that?"

"Because he is a guru, a guide in spiritual things."

But something did not quite fit so I pursued the matter by asking, "And what chance event has brought him here?"

"Oh, it is a long story," she said carelessly. "He has led a wandering life."

She became pensive.

"Some nights ago I dreamed a deadly dream about these hanging trees in this dread passage."

Speaking slowly like one who had been hypnotized, she intoned, "How dark it is in this cool avenue and how the great branches shoot across the sky blacking out the stars. If you were to crouch low on one of those gnarled tree limbs you could drop down on the back of anyone who passed and they would never know that you were there until they felt your fingers on their throat."

I was almost as shocked as when she had cried, 'Kill Plumet.'

"What a horrible idea," I exclaimed.

"Gloomy places always give me gloomy thoughts," she said sadly. "By the way, I want you to do me a favor, Dr. Garzon."

"What is that?" I asked.

"Don't say anything at the house about

that poor compatriot of mine. They might think of him as a rogue and a vagabond you know and order him to be driven from the village."

"I'm sure Dr. Conn would do nothing so unkind, Miss Songana. It's not his form."

"No, but Mr. Plumet might."

"That's possible so just as you like," I said. "But the children are sure to tell."

"No, I think not," she answered.

I don't know how she managed to curb their little prattling tongues but she did exercise some magnetic power over them. Was it fear or devotion? They certainly preserved silence upon the point and there was no talk that evening of the visitor from the past who had appeared so suddenly in our little hamlet.

Once alone in my chambers, I read the telegram from O'Neill again. It had come as one of the great shocks in my life. But I resolved to follow my friend's instruction to the letter and spy on the governess and Plumet.

I had a shrewd suspicion that the strange guru from the tropics was no chance wanderer but had come to Seaview upon some set errand.

Next day I had the best possible evidence that he was still in the vicinity, for

I met Miss Songana coming down the garden walk with a basketful of bread, fruit and meat in her hand. The viands looked good.

"Is this for delivery to Juan Gallegos or is it for a picnic that I can join in?" I asked.

"Neither one nor the other," she said, with a smile. "I'll tell you the truth, Dr. Garzon, because you have always been a good friend to me and I feel that I can trust you. These choice pieces are for my master guru. I'll hang the basket here on this branch and he will get it."

"Oh, he's still about then," I observed.

"Yes, he's still in the neighborhood."

"You think he will find it?" I asked.

"Oh, trust him for that," she said. "You don't blame me for helping him do you? You would do the same if you lived among Orientals and suddenly came upon a Christian cleric. Come to the hothouse with me and look at the flowers."

We walked around to the conservatory together and talked awhile. When we came back, the basket was still hanging onto the branch but the contents were gone. Incongruously, two dead sparrows and a dead crow lay on the ground nearby. I must admit that I failed to understand the meaning or symbolism of this act of apparent ceremonial desecration. Miss Songana took the basket down with a desperate gaze all around and carried it into the kitchen with her.

It seemed to me that since the encounter with the dark guru the day before her spirits had become more subdued and her step less free and less elastic. It may have been my imagination, but it appeared to me also that she was not as constrained as usual in the presence of Plumet and that she met his glances more fearlessly and was less under the influence of his will.

And now I am coming to that part of this narration of mine which describes how I first gained an insight into the relationship which existed between those two mysterious mortals.

I learned the terrible truth about Miss Songana or of the Priestess Songana as I should prefer to call her. For assuredly she was the true descendant of the fierce fanatical mutineer more than of her gentle Anglo-speaking mother. And for me these following revelations came as a shock, the effect of which I shall never forget.

CHAPTER TWENTY

A Student of Eavesdropping

Felix O'Neill gets Garzon to spy on Miss Songana and Plumet.

It is possible in the way in which I have told this story that my readers have already detected the cultural demons which seemed to torment Miss Songana. I have been emphasizing those facts which had a bearing upon her and omitting those which had not.

As for myself, I solemnly aver that up to the last moment I had not the smallest suspicion of the truth. Little did I know what manner of woman this was, whose hand I pressed in friendship and whose voice was music to my ears. Yet it was my deranged belief, at that time, that she was really well disposed to me and would not willingly have harmed me. That night, I set out to follow O'Neill's instructions.

It was in this manner that the revelations came out. I think I have already mentioned that there was a certain arbor in the shrubbery in which I was accustomed to read during the daytime. It was also known to me that in this secluded grotto Plumet and Miss Songana were wont to meet in the evenings as O'Neill had reminded me in his strange telegram.

At about ten o'clock, acting on my friend's instructions, I went to the summer-house giving the impression that I intended to do a couple of hours writing before turning in.

Dr. Conn and the children and the servants had already gone to bed. I slipped downstairs very quietly and turned the key gently in the front door. Once in the open air I hurried rapidly across the lawn and so into the shrubbery with the intention of listening to a private conversation, that is to say, eavesdropping.

I overheard the pleasant sound of the crickets and the birds chattering to each other above the whispering of the trees on this hot balmy June evening. But soon I was to hear less innocent talk than that of the birds.

I had hardly passed the little wooden gate and entered the plantation before I heard the sound of talking and knew that I had chanced to stumble upon one of those nocturnal conclaves which I had sometimes observed from my window. The voices were those of the secretary and of the governess.

It was clear to me from the direction in which the voices came that they were sitting in the arbor and conversing together without any suspicion of the presence of a third person.

I have ever held that to eavesdrop on a private conversation under any but the most extreme circumstances is a dishonorable practice.

As O'Neill once wittily remarked to me, What people say to each other in the privacy and security of their own homes should be strictly between themselves and of course the government. Therefore, I knew that the astonishing O'Neill must have had good reasons for asking me to do this.

Soon I heard some words from Plumet that brought me to a halt with every faculty of my being overwhelmed with horrified amazement.

"Set fire to the west wing and I will drug their late night drink to make sure the old man, the children and the doltish healtharian researcher will all breathe in the smoke. Old houses easily catch fire. It will look like they died by accident and I will have no trouble with the inheritance since I am the sole beneficiary of the will. There will be no reason to suspect you of this act and I will be careful to create a full-proof alibi for myself elsewhere."

These were the words I heard sounding clearly and distinctly through the warm humid night air. Shocking words in the incisive tones of the amanuensis.

I stood breathless, listening with all my ears. My every thought was intently focused on gaining some knowledge, some way to circumvent or foil the arsonly crime which these grotesque conspirators were hatching upon this still summer night.

I heard the deep, sweet tones of her voice but she spoke so rapidly and in such a subdued manner that it was difficult to understand exactly what was being said. But I could tell by her intonation that she was under the influence of deep emotion.

The moon was not yet rising. Under the shadows of the trees it was very dark so that there was little chance of my being observed. I drew nearer on tiptoe, with my ears straining to catch every sound.

"Eaten his bread, indeed," said the secretary derisively. "You are not usually so squeamish. You did not think of that in the case of little Deirdre."

"I was mad. Yes, I was mad to steal the sacred lamp and the book of wisdom," she ejaculated in a broken voice. "I had prayed much to Yeti and it seemed to me that in this land of unbelievers, my mother's land, it would be a great and glorious thing for me a lonely woman to act up to the teachings of Yeti.

"There are few women who have ever been admitted into the secrets of our faith, and it was but by an accident of birth being born to my father, a priest, that the honor came upon me. Yet, having once had the path pointed out to me I have walked straight and fearlessly. The high priest of our faith has said that even in my fourteenth year I was worthy to sit upon the steps of the great teaching hall.

"Yet I swear by the sacred lamp that I have grieved much over this, for what had the poor child Deirdre done that she should be sacrificed. I had to appease the spirits of evil from whom I had stolen the book and lamp. I had to kill to expiate my sins of stealing and lies and fleeing from justice. I fear that I am still being stalked by the Yeti fanatics."

"I fancy that your regrets have been caused more by your being found out by yours truly than by any moral aspect of the case," Plumet said, with a sneer. "I may have had my suspicions about you before, but it was only when I saw you rising up smiling from the body of the child, as you held a vial of poison in your hand, that I knew for certain that we were honored by the presence of a priestess of Yeti the Abominable Snowman. A foreign scaffold would be rather a prosaic end for such a distinguished servant of the Yeti.

"Here in the Celtcountry there has always been the pagan worship of the giant hound. I would like to know if you came here to join with other diabolical druidic priests who are suspected to be still concocting their child murders and animal sacrifices in this ancient domain of the Grayreaper."

"That is not for you to know for you would use your knowledge to extort all that you could out of me," she said bitterly. "You have certainly made my existence a burden to me and done your best to exploit me."

"Extort. Exploit. A burden to you," he rasped, in an altered voice. "You know what my feelings are towards you. If I have occasionally governed you by the fear of exposure it was only because I found you were insensible to the milder influence of my utter devotion to you."

"Devotion," she cried, bitterly. "How repulsive an emotion. But let us come to the point Mr. Plumet. You promise me my unconditional liberty if I do this one last thing for you?"

"Yes," answered Plumet. "I just want to inherit the estate and to wipe out the other potential heirs. After that, you may go where you wish. I shall forget that I saw you here in the shrubbery giving the child a potion which at once tormented it into a screaming death. I shall forget where you hide the lamp and book at night. I will remember only that you read from the book by the light of the sacred lamp to guide your soul to its destiny."

"The authorities would never believe your accusations but to keep the sacred lamp and the book of wisdom I would do anything," she said, "though I doubt if anyone would ever believe that I am the adept of a faith that sacrifices children to appease black powers."

"Well it's true," said Plumet, "truth is stranger than fiction. Only the good believe the truth but there are some good men in authority around this our old Celtcountry. They just might believe me."

CHAPTER TWENTY ONE
The Murder Plot

The plot thickens as Plumet and Miss Songana refine details of the pact between them. Garzon wonders how to save the O'Neill family?

"Steel yourself. You should know that we can never have such a chance again to get wealth," Plumet cried. "Felix O'Neill is away and that healtharian friend of his sleeps heavily and is too stupid to suspect anything. The will is made out in my favor, and if the old man and the children die, every stick and stone of the great estate will be mine and yours too if you will join me."

"Why don't you do it yourself, then?" she asked bitterly. "It's easy to start a fire."

"It's not in my line," he said. "Besides I have not got the knack of greed - the root of evil - or whatever you call it.

"As the doctor's heir I would be the prime suspect if someone had seen me nearby at the time of the fire. So I'll sleep in the gate lodge. The servants will no doubt witness to my being there.

"Besides, I'll be poisoning the latenight drinks of the O'Neill family. You may be proud to know that I will be using the powder that you so kindly gave to me. That will be quite enough to wipe out the whole clan. Ah yes, the poison that you use to kill children leaves little or no trace. That's the beauty of it."

"It is an accursed thing to slay one's benefactor," Songana muttered sulkily.

"But it is a great thing to serve the priestess of the Yeti," said Plumet, "she who leads to death and she who sends souls into their long home. I know enough about your religion to recognize that much. Surely your father would have done it if he had been here?"

"My father was the greatest of all the philosophers of death," she said, sadly. "He has set free into death more souls than there are days in the decade."

"I wouldn't have met him for a thousand pounds," Plumet remarked, with a laugh and a flash of his old wit. "But what would such a deep philosopher say now if he saw his daughter hesitate with such a chance before her of serving the souls of men and women? So far you have done excellently. He may well have smiled when the infant soul of young Deirdre was wafted up to this goal of yours."

Plumet's voice acquired a hard, gritty edge. "Perhaps this is not the first sacrifice you have made. How about the daughter of that charitable Sailport merchant? What of your early days as a young priestess? Ah, I see in your face that I am right once again. After such deeds, you do wrong to hesitate when there is no danger and especially now that all will be made easy for you. Besides that, the deed will free you from your existence here which cannot be particularly pleasant. This would be like a rope so to speak hanging around your neck the whole time - if you get my meaning."

I could hear a gasping shudder from Songana's lips.

"If this is to be done it must be done at once," Plumet continued. "The old man might rewrite his will at any moment for he is fond of the children and he is as changeable as a weathercock. Even that wily and cunning fox or should I say beagle, Felix O'Neill, might find out something suspicious about you or I, Miss Murderess. What a horrible thought."

There was a long pause and a silence so profound that I seemed to hear my own heart throbbing in the darkness.

"When do you think it should be done?" she asked at last.

"Why not tomorrow night, the sooner the better?" suggested Plumet.

"How and where am I to light the fire?" Miss Songana asked.

Plumet explained his plan. "I want you to set fire to Felix's room. From there the fire will spread. Remember that he's away at the moment so that you'll not be interrupted. I've unlocked his room which is directly underneath the old man's room. Also, I shall leave Dr. Conn's door open if I can so that the smoke will drift upwards. It will drift through the creaking cracks and crevices and choke the old man and the children. It will not matter if the dumb healtharian dies or not. He has even less claim on the estate than the remote cousin, Felix, nor is he clever enough to appeal to the old man's sense of meritocracy and fair shares.

"Dr. Conn sleeps heavily and I shall leave a night-light burning in the hall so that you may see your way out."

"And afterwards?" she asked.

"Afterwards you will briefly return to the house. Then raise the alarm and run out. It will be discovered that our poor employer has passed away in the fire. It will also be found that he has left all his worldly goods as a slight return for the devoted labors of his faithful secretary a Mr. Plumet who generously rewards the now redundant governess and tutor. Then the services of the newly rich governess, Miss Songana, being no longer required, she may go back to her beloved country or to anywhere else that she fancies. If she so pleases, she can run away with Dr. Arturo Garzon, a slow-witted researcher of healthics."

"You insult me," she said angrily and then, after a pause, "you must meet me tomorrow night before I give the alarm."

"Why so?" he asked.

"Because nothing ever works perfectly. There may be some snag, some unforeseen difficulty on which I may require help and guidance."

"Ah yes, the best laid schemes of mice and men gang aft agley, as Garzon likes to quote and very truly. Very well then, let us meet here at twelve," he agreed.

"No, not here. It is too near the house. Let us meet under the great oak at the head of the avenue. You can get there and back to your lodge more easily and not be seen."

"Wherever you want," he answered, sulkily, "but mind, I am the heir and the natural suspect. I need an alibi. Villagers will see the light in the lodge and our servants will know where I am. So I'm not going to be with you when you do it."

"I shall not ask you to be with me," she said, scornfully. "I think we have said all that needs to be said about this matter."

Then I heard the sound of one or other of them rising to their feet and though they continued to talk I did not stop to listen. Instead, I crept quietly out from my place of concealment and scudded across the dark lawn and in through the door which I closed behind me. It was only when I had regained my room and locked my little suite of chambers and had sunk back into my armchair that I was able to collect my scattered senses and think over the terrible conversation that I had just overheard.

Long into the wee hours of the night I sat motionless and stunned as I meditated over every word that I had heard. I was endeavoring to form in my mind some plan of action for the next twenty-four hours.

CHAPTER TWENTY TWO
Fanaticism

Deeper and darker details of the plot begin to emerge as Garzon puts together his rescue plan.

I thought carefully about the dangers of the situation and could not at first determine what to do. It was to say the least, a confusing dilemma.

Evidently Plumet had seen Songana give the little Deirdre a drink before the child had the fatal fit. Clearly he had been unsure at first if the drink had caused the child's death so he kept quiet and brooded.

He had somehow gained access to the book of wisdom while Miss Songana was busy tutoring the children. Apparently he had been able to translate and understand the despicable instructions concerning child sacrifice supposedly to appease the powers of darkness and to gain worldly success.

No doubt from this and other clues Plumet had correctly concluded that Miss Songana was a multiple child-killer and he was now blackmailing her for his nefarious purposes. But was she the killer?

One of the first children whom she had tutored in Sailport had apparently been murdered there by a self-confessed killer. Surely this beggar, even though he was now behind bars, must have had something to do with the murder of little Deirdre O'Neill? And what of this killer's mystical crew of Sailport supporters just a few miles away?

I was in an agony as to how to save the old man and the two surviving children. If I warned Dr. Conn, his manner could alert the conspirators. This might cause them to smell a rat and then put in place some alternative homicidal plan about which I would know nothing. A plan that I could not hope to thwart.

I was also totally confused about Miss Songana's guilt or innocence. Sometimes I believed her guilty and the next moment I was certain of her innocence. Was there any possibility that Plumet's accusations would be proven false?

Perhaps some subtle oriental drug or perfume, well known to Plumet, had been used to hallucinate and delude Miss Songana. This may have caused her sense of self-guilt to be based only on false memory, mesmerism, mindmadness and thought manipulation. These were all well known techniques of the occult as well as delusion and insanity.

Perhaps the real villains were the shadowy devotees of the Yeti whose unholy book and lamp had apparently influenced Miss Songana.

On the other hand, Miss Songana may indeed have been the perpetrator of murder. For that matter I had heard her admit as much to Plumet.

Also, I had read rumors about wild fanatics who are found in the remote parts of the east and whose distorted religion represents murder as being the highest and purest of all the gifts which a mortal can offer up.

I well remember an account of such devotees. It talked about their secrecy, their organization, their relentlessness and the terrible power which their homicidal craze has over every mental or moral faculty.

It was quite possible that a sacred lamp and book were the tools with which they were wont to guide their demon-appeasing purpose.

Songana had already been a grown woman when she had left their community. She had told me that she was the daughter of their principal leader. Therefore, it was no wonder that the varnish of civilization had not eradicated all her early impressions or prevented the breaking out of occasional fits of fanaticism.

Apparently, in one of these fits she had put an end to little Deirdre O'Neill. Then she had carefully prepared an alibi in order to conceal her crime.

It was Plumet's accidental discovery of this murder that gave him such power over his mysterious associate.

With very few exceptions, it is common among religious communities to find that those who encourage the death and suicide of others are not themselves much given over to applying the idea to themselves.

Miss Songana realized that she had subjected herself to death by the law of our land. This could be the reason why she had found herself compelled to suppress her will and tame her imperious nature when in the presence of the amanuensis. I simply could not make up my mind about Miss Songana even though the evidence was clear that she was indeed a child killer.

A great horror and loathing filled my whole being when I thought over what Plumet had done and what he proposed to do. Was this his return to his employer for the kindness lavished upon him by the learned professor? He had already cozened the scholarly old doctor into signing away his estates but this was not enough for the pen-pusher.

Now, for fear that some prickings of conscience should cause the old man to change his mind, Plumet had determined to put it out of Dr. Conn's power ever to write a codicil.

All this was bad enough but the acme of it all seemed to be that he was too cowardly to effect his purpose with his own hand.

Instead he made use of Miss Songana's strange misconceptions about religion. This would remove Dr. Conn in such a way that no suspicion could possibly fall upon the real culprit.

I determined in my mind that come what may the amanuensis would not escape from the punishment due for his crimes.

But what was I to do? Had I known of O'Neill's address I would have telegraphed for him in the morning and he could have been back in Seaview before nightfall.

Unfortunately O'Neill was the worst of correspondents when he was engrossed in intellectual work. Although he had been gone for some days we had received no word yet of his whereabouts since his last telegram mentioned only the Capital as his address.

There were three maidservants in the house but no man, with the exception of old Harry. I did not know of anyone in the neighborhood upon whom I could rely with the possible exception of mine host in the village. This however was a small matter for I knew that in personal strength I was more than a match for Plumet. I had enough confidence in myself to feel that my resistance alone would be sufficient to prevent any possibility of the full plot being carried out.

The question was, what were the best steps to take under the circumstances? My first impulse was to wait until morning, then to quietly go or to send to the nearest police-station and summon a couple of constables. I could then place Plumet and his female accomplice into the hands of justice and narrate the conversation which I had overheard.

On second thoughts this plan struck me as being a very impracticable one. What grain of evidence had I against them, except my story?

To people who did not know me, this tale would certainly appear to be a very wild and improbable one.

Also, I could well imagine the plausible voice and imperturbable manner with which the college-educated Plumet would oppose the accusation and how he would dilate upon the ill-will which I bore both him and his companion on account of their mutual affection.

How easy it would be for him to make a third person believe that I was trumping up a story in the hope of injuring a rival. And how difficult it would be for me to make anyone believe that this clerical-looking gentleman and this stylishly-dressed lady were two beasts of prey who were hunting in couples. I felt that it would be a great mistake for me to show my hand before I was sure of the game.

The alternative was to say nothing and to let things take their course, being always ready to step in when the evidence against the conspirators appeared to be conclusive.

In the meantime I would need to think of some excuse to keep Dr. Conn and the young children safely locked away from flame and fumes.

This was the course which tentatively recommended itself to my adventurous disposition. It also appeared to be the one most likely to lead to successful results.

CHAPTER TWENTY THREE

A Long Day

Garzon attempts to foil the plans of the two conspirators and to secure the safety of the O'Neill family.

That night I slept little. My mind felt like it had bled profusely and had then been cauterized with a crude red hot poker.

The thought of the murderous plot obsessed and tormented me. It presented many dilemmas so divided and twisted were my thoughts about the lovely oriental governess.

At last at early dawn I stretched myself upon my bed. By then I had fully made up my mind to retain my knowledge of the murderous intrigue in my own breast. I had decided to trust myself entirely for the defeat of the treacherous plot which I had overheard the night before.

Old Dr. Conn was in high spirits next morning after breakfast and insisted upon reading aloud from his great compendium of eastern remedies.

Plumet sat silent and inscrutable by his side, save when he threw in a suggestion or uttered an exclamation of admiration.

Miss Songana appeared to be lost in thought and it seemed to me more than once that I saw a determined glint in her dark eyes.

It was frightening for me to watch the three of them drinking tea in company and to think of the real relationship in which they stood with each other.

How many other breakfasters or diners or convivial drinkers were similarly plotting to kill each other? Perhaps more than we shall ever know.

My heart warmed towards the children and my little red-faced host with the quaint eastern headgear and his old-fashioned churchgoing ways. I vowed to myself that no harm should befall them while I had power to prevent it. How I wished that Felix O'Neill had been present at this time.

That day wore along slowly and drearily. It was impossible for me to settle down to work so I wandered restlessly about the corridors of the old shambling house and around the garden.

I saw little of Plumet that day as he spent most of the time upstairs working with Dr. Conn.

Twice when I was striding up and down in the garden I perceived the governess coming with the children in my direction, but on each occasion I avoided her by hurrying away among the moving breezy greenery and the sunny shadows of the trees.

I felt that I could not speak to her without showing the intense horror with which she had lately inspired me. In this case I might have betrayed my knowledge of what had transpired the night before, whatever the truth might be about Miss Songana.

She noticed that I shunned her. For at luncheon, when my eyes caught hers for a moment, she flashed across a surprised and injured glance at me. However, I made no response to this but rather thought it curious that one so cruel and selfish, indeed murderous, should feel hurt or offended at so little as my discourtesy.

Or was it that she was innocent of the crimes attributed to her and she sought my help? Or was it more subtle, that she was guilty but had repented and hated herself for what she had become? What were her real feelings towards me? At that time I could not read the deep secrets of her mind nor can I now.

At last, the afternoon post brought a letter from my friend Felix O'Neill telling us that he was stopping at the Victoria Hotel.

I knew that it was now impossible for him to be of any use to me in the way of sharing the responsibility for whatever might occur. Nevertheless, I thought it my duty to telegraph him and let him know that his presence was desirable.

This involved a long walk to the station but that was useful as it helped me to while away the time. When I heard the clicking of the needles which told me that my message was flying upon its way, I felt a great weight lift off my mind.

When I reached the avenue gate on my return from Seaview village, I found our old serving-man Harry standing there. He was apparently in a violent passion.

"They says as one rat brings others," he said to me, touching his hat, "and it seems as it be the same with they Orientals."

He had always disliked the governess on account of what he called her foreign talk.

I reminded the old groom that there are many shapes, sizes and complexions but there is only one race - humanity - for the good lord has made of one blood all the peoples of the earth as it says in the good book.

He merely grunted resentfully at my lecture or was it a sermon?

"So what's the matter then?" I asked.

"It's two o' they furriners a-hidin' and a-prowlin'," said the old man. "I seed them here among the bushes and I sent them off wi' a bit o' my mind. Lookin' after the hens as like as not, or maybe wantin' to burn the house and murder us all in our beds."

I gasped at his chance hit.

"I'll go down to village Dr. Garzon and see what they're after," as he hurried away down the road in a paroxysm of fear, anger and xenophobia.

This little incident made a considerable impression on me and I thought seriously about it as I walked up the long avenue. It was clear that the wandering Orientals were still hanging around the premises. They were factors whom I had forgotten to take into account.

If their sophisticated compatriot, Miss Songana, enlisted them as accomplices in her dark plans, it was possible that a total of four assailants – Plumet, Songana and two Orientals - might be too many for me to deal with. Still, it appeared to me to be improbable that she should do so, since she had taken such pains to conceal from Plumet the presence of one of her fellow countrymen – the mysterious Fakir.

For lack of help I was half tempted to take Harry into my confidence but on second thoughts I came to the conclusion that a man of his frailty would be worse than useless as an ally. However, fate gave me a chance.

At about seven o'clock that evening, I was restlessly lurking near the kitchen. Suddenly I was approached by Plumet who conspicuously asked me, within hearing of the three ancient maidservants, whether I could tell him where Miss Songana was. I answered that I had not seen her.

Plumet, anxious for an alibi, asked me to take some bedtime drinks which he had prepared to the others. I agreed and Plumet hurried on with an agitated and disturbed expression on his features.

Quickly I switched the poisoned cups for harmless cocoa and took them to the old man and the children in the hall.

Then I borrowed the keys from the kitchen, locked Felix's room and checked that all other west wing rooms were locked. Next, I searched Plumet's and Songana's rooms for hidden weapons or firearms but found none. I then set up a vigil.

Now, in the absence of both Songana and Plumet, I was able to warn Dr. Conn and the children to be sure to lock and bar themselves in the Doctor's suite that night due to the known presence of foreign prowlers in the grounds of the estate. Dr. Conn heartily agreed for the nervous children's sake.

Miss Songana's absence did not seem a matter of surprise to me. No doubt she was out in the shrubbery somewhere collecting tinder wood to start the fire. She was also gathering together her courage and nerving herself for the terrible piece of work that she had undertaken to do.

I closed my door behind me and sat down with a book in my hand but with my mind still too much excited to comprehend the contents. My precise plan of campaign had now been formed.

CHAPTER TWENTY FOUR
Rough Justice

The plotters find that their deadly plan has been challenged and Felix returns from the Capital.

It is odd how certain events in our lives set a pattern for later happenings. Such presentiments or foreshadowings seem to defy scientific explanation.

Perhaps our physical strength and reflexes, our mental powers or limitations provide biological parameters within which we are confined for better or worse.

Perhaps we all have been allocated celestial numbers that describe our fate like statistics.

Again, we all try to do the things that bring us success, the things we are good at. Or maybe it is fate or destiny that calls us to follow our pilgrim roads. I do not know.

Healthics, not philosophy, is my field but I do know that the events set out in this chapter proved to be seminal towards a long harvest for both my friend Felix O'Neill and I over a period of many years.

I do not remember any period of my life when the hours passed so slowly. I will always recall that night in my room that overlooked mistily and at a distance, the shrubbery, the trysting place and the great oak trees across the lawn.

Faraway I heard the mellow tones of the Seaview clock as it struck the hours of eight and then of nine. There seemed to be an interminable pause before the striking of ten. After that it seemed as though time had stopped altogether. I paced up and down in my little suite of rooms fearing and yet longing for the hour, as men will, when some great ordeal is about to fall upon them.

However, all things have an end. At last there came pealing through the still night air the first clear stroke which announced the eleventh, the one before the appointed twelfth hour of death - the final deadline of the killers.

Then I arose and, putting on my soft slippers, seized my stick and slipped quietly out of my rooms and down the creaking old-fashioned staircase.

I could hear the stertorous snoring of Dr. Conn coming from the floor above with the children locked in his suite of rooms by our prior agreement. I had had no problem in persuading him to hide since he was aware of prowlers seen in the grounds by old Harry and others.

Just before 11:30 that evening I began to patrol the corridors. I smelled something burning and suddenly a gasping Miss Songana brushed pass. I do not believe she even saw me. I followed the smell of smoke and sure enough discovered a fire on the landing outside Felix's room to which she had been unable to gain access. Felix's room was just below Dr. Conn's locked room. Silently, I grabbed a nearby firedouse bucket and put out the flames without any trouble.

Of course, the plotters were under the impression that Dr. Conn and his natural heirs had been poisoned. Nevertheless I was determined, no matter what, not to allow the lady to approach Felix's room or set a fire again.

I then followed Miss Songana's steps and determined to be within sight of both the murderous plotters and their trysting-place. I would follow them and interfere at any moment when my interference would have some effect such as an attempt to rekindle a fire.

I had chosen from among my walking sticks, a thick, knobby stick dear to my hiker's heart and with this I knew that I was master of the situation since my search had ascertained that the plotters had no knives, darts or hidden firearms.

I managed to feel my way to the front door through the darkness and, having opened it, passed out into the clear dome of the starlit night. It was unhealthily warm and clammy. A stiff wind started up and I felt a few cold splatters of raindrop on my face.

I had to be very careful of my movements because at first the moon shone so brightly that it was almost as light as day. I hugged the shadow of the house until I reached the garden hedge. Then crawling down in its shelter I found myself safe in the shrubbery where I had been eavesdropping the night before. Through this I made my way, treading very cautiously and gingerly so that not a stick snapped beneath my feet.

In this way I advanced until I found myself among the brushwood at the edge of the plantation and within full view of the great oak-tree which stood at the upper end of the avenue of trees, like a huge Viking seafarer at the head of his navy.

There was someone standing under the shadow of the oak. At first I could hardly make out who it was but presently the figure began to move and, coming out into a silvery patch where the moon shone down between two branches, looked impatiently to the left and to the right. Then I saw that it was Plumet who was waiting alone. The governess apparently had not yet kept her appointment.

It was early summer and a sudden thunderstorm had begun to flash and send trees crashing with rain and darkness. It was one of those malicious storms when the Grayreaper, the devil, seems to crack his whip over the earth showing utter contempt for rich or poor, the old, the sick, the terrified.

As I wished to hear as well as to see, I wormed my way along under the dark shadows of the trunks in the direction of the huge oak. When I stopped I was not more than fifteen paces from the spot where the tall gaunt figure of the amanuensis looked grim and ghastly in the shifting light from clear to dark. He paced about uneasily, now disappearing into the shadows, now reappearing in the silvery patches where the lightning broke through the covering above him.

It was evident from his movements that he was puzzled and disconcerted at the non-appearance of his accomplice. Finally he stationed himself under a great branch which concealed his figure. From beneath it he commanded a view of the gravel drive which led down from the house. Along this path he no doubt expected Miss Songana to come.

This she eventually did. She walked very slowly on her deadly tryst and I could see that she turned around frequently to stare at the west wing windows. No doubt she was looking in vain for the flames of a fatal fire. Thunder clapped so that I could not hear any conversation.

I lay quietly in my hiding-place, a little wet but congratulating myself inwardly at having gained a vantage point from which I could see all without risk of discovery. Suddenly my eye lit upon something which made my heart rise to my mouth. It almost caused me to utter an ejaculation which would have betrayed my presence.

A long lean black shadow sprang out of the shades towards me. At first my heart leapt in my chest and I feared that the shadow was of the same build as the village guru.

"Shush, relax old chap," said the shadow.

To my utter surprise it was my friend Felix O'Neill. My heart calmed down as I recovered myself and we both surveyed the scene of the murder plot.

I have said that Plumet, now joined by Miss Songana, was standing immediately under one of the great branches of the oak-tree. Beneath this all was plunged in the deepest shadow but the upper part of the branch itself was silvered over by the light of the storm.

As I gazed I became conscious that down this luminous branch things were crawling and flickering. These appeared to be shapeless somethings that were almost indistinguishable from the branch itself. They were slowly and steadily writhing their way along it.

As I watched, my eyes became more accustomed to the light and then these indefinite somethings took some form and substance.

They appeared to be oriental humans - men - but short and stocky - not like the Indian whom I had seen in the village. With their arms and legs twined around the great limb they were shuffling their way down as silently and almost as rapidly as one of their native snakes.

Before I had time to conjecture the meaning of their presence they were directly over the spot where the secretary and Miss

Songana stood.

O'Neill and I could clearly see these attackers with their bronzed bodies clad only in loin cloths. They were showing up hard and clear against the erratic disc of moonlight behind them. Occasionally they were lit up by stabs of lightning.

I saw them take something from around their waists. They hesitated for a moment as though judging the distance. Then they sprang downwards and crashed through the intervening foliage.

There were screams and heavy thuds as of several bodies falling together. Then there arose on the night air a noise as of someone gargling his throat followed by a succession of croaking sounds.

I shall always remember the sounds from that night. Indeed, they will haunt me to my dying day.

There were two assassins, or should I say counter-assassins, both dropping from the great oak; one springing out from the nearby bushes like a tiger and the other falling from the tree directly on his female victim like a snake. They had made no mistakes in their meticulous work.

Following O'Neill, who was first on the spot, I saw that the skeletal amanuensis and the governess lay dead. The woman had evidently tried to escape but had been stopped. It required very little knowledge of healthics to determine as much. Both of their throats had been deeply and cleanly slashed like animals in a slaughterhouse. The blood was everywhere.

O'Neill was looking around the area and following his gaze I saw two silent shadows entering the great hallway of Seaview House.

As we rushed to the main entrance we heard the screams of the servants. When we entered the great hall, old Harry pointed dumbly towards the library and we heard the sounds of breaking glass.

By the time we entered the library the book of wisdom and the sacred lamp were gone, the back window of the library had been smashed open and the sound of horses hooves was echoing from the back lawn.

Obviously the two avengers had been watching and planning over a period of time and had learned to identify where the lamp and book were likely to be found. Then they had carefully prepared their escape route with horses.

O'Neill looked around and saw only the servants. As we rushed back to the great hall again he paused and grabbed me by the lapels, "The children and Uncle Conn, where are they? How are they Garzon, for heaven's sake what has become of them?"

"Relax O'Neill, I have them locked since early on in Dr. Conn's rooms. I made the excuse of prowlers being spotted so as not to have Dr. Conn confront the secretary or Miss Songana, with disastrous results no doubt."

O'Neill pounded my shoulder so hard it almost hurt. "Good man, Garzon, I knew I could rely on you. Wonderful. You're the very chap I'd like to have with me in any tight corner. That's why I sent you the warning wire. What was their plot? Long knives?"

I shook my head. "Not for their first choice. They planned poison, then fire and smoke inhalation to confuse the cause. I was able to switch the bedtime drinks to something harmless - a light sedative to be exact. Later I was able to dowse the fire."

Once again O'Neill slapped my back and began to shake my hand with intense power. "Great work, well held, Garzon old chap. It was pure inspiration on my part to invite you here. My family owe you their lives."

"Thank you, O'Neill. I do try to keep a stiff upper lip, as you know."

I was pleased and gratified to hear O'Neill's praise which is praise indeed.

"I'll be happy to help out any time," I stammered.

That night was a bad night for harmony. Ugly storm music roared over the harsh moors and bushes were blasted by howling winds. Monsters seemed to crawl out of the meres. Spirits cried out in pain from the swamps and rose out of holes in the ground while dogs howled in agony as lightning struck and crashed down trees. The Grayreaper screamed in the elements. Mists whirled around as the rain dried up in the thirsty ground.

After confirming that Dr. Conn and the children were safe and well, we drove to the telegraph office. There we awakened the railway stationmaster and sent telegrams to alert the various authorities.

We had an unpleasant suspicion that the well organized oriental assassins would not easily be caught. Two bloodstained loin cloths were found about a mile from the village. No doubt these visiting malcreants assumed respectable disguises which they had previously hidden in their saddle bags.

It was suspected afterwards that the oriental killers had caught an early Fiersley train from the local station and were safe in our great Imperial metropolis before any real search could be made for them. Their two horses were found abandoned at the Fiersley railway station and were returned to their rightful owner, a farmer who had reported them stolen.

The messengers of death who had kept a longtime tryst from afar under the old oak-tree were never either heard of nor seen again.

At first there was a hue and cry over the whole countryside but of course nothing came of it. Probably the fugitives passed their days in cheap hotels and traveled rapidly at night, living on throwaway scraps until they caught a ship bound for some faroff port of our vast Eastern Empire.

Concerning Songana and Plumet, as O'Neill said at the time, he had arrived too late to save our two household villains for formal justice but not too late to witness them getting their just desserts.

Indeed, we had here a type of poetic justice since the two plotters died before they could carry out any more of their kill-for-greed plans and received full retribution for their past blackmail and murders.

I often wonder how it is possible for such debased, perhaps insane, malefactors to live an outwardly respectable existence, sometimes masquerading as decent church-going people. Yet, at the same time, these people lead a second and hidden life of murder and greed behind the lace curtains of convention. Are there, here among us, more such masqueraders than we realize?

Do we really ever find out about most of the secret crimes concealed behind the closed doors and shutters of unsuspected murdercraft?

Does this explain the occasional sudden disasters that befall some people so suddenly and so sadly? Falls? Tumbling down stairs? Slips in the bathroom? Food poisoning? Road accidents? Leaving home unexpectedly, never to return? And are these disasters crimes by close relatives and friends or are they, in some cases, the opposite – retribution from an outraged moral eternity? We can only gaze and gape in horror. Who can tell?

I remembered reading somewhere that all good or evil deeds and thoughts fly out into space, bounce off the far wall of the universe and return to hit the perpetrator with four times the power. In other words, what goes around comes around, often with increased impact.

Yet perhaps even Miss Songana, having foreseen in her strange dream the possible death of Plumet and herself, had nevertheless deliberately led both him and herself to their doom that night at the dark and drooping oak tree. Why? Acceptance? Repentance? Remorse? True Love of Death? Who Knows?

Ah, Miss Songana.

CHAPTER TWENTY FIVE
Light from the Sacred Lamp

Garzon and O'Neill have dinner at the nearby Anglo-Hispanic hostelry and discuss the whole case in detail over a good meal.

I had the painful duty of explaining to Dr. Conn the entire background to the events of that fateful day. It may have occurred to him that he had been over-dedicated to his writing. This had resulted in him being too trustful of Miss Songana and Plumet. Felix O'Neill decided not to involve the local authorities in the matter any further than was necessary.

Plumet and Miss Songana were buried as victims of oriental prowlers. These suspicious characters had been seen occasionally and fleetingly on the nearby cliffs, although never in the town itself. Even the county police have never known the full story of that strange tragedy and they certainly never shall unless, indeed, the eyes of some of them should chance to fall upon this narrative.

The remains of Plumet and Miss Songana were buried quietly in the old parish churchyard of St. Thomas in Seaview Village. Few mourners showed up except the Vicar, O'Neill and myself. I later heard that her grave lay undisturbed for many moonlights.

Dr. Conn gave the four old servants fully paid compassionate home leave, a generous and humane gesture that was typical of the man's truly Imperial sense of fair play.

After making out a will to bequeath Cormac the entire estate and a fixed life income for little Doreen, the good doctor had wisely taken the children away for a summer holiday. He decided to take them to St. Malo, supposedly to improve their French but really to ease them away from the turmoil of the funeral and the terror of their tutor's guilt.

Before he left, Dr. Conn had begged me to accept a large cash reward for saving his life but of course I had to refuse on the grounds that a gentleman should never accept payment for doing his duty.

The old doctor sighed deeply and shook his head but accepted my decision with a good and cheerful grace and a heartfelt shake of the hand.

"You're welcome here anytime, Garzon, my dear fellow," he had assured me.

No doubt he was still in white sun helmet and riding boots, repudiating himself vigorously as an ogre of sneeze, cough, spit, hot air and repulsive old age, much to the amusement of Cormac and Doreen.

Dr. Conn was an intelligent and congenial if eccentric and obsessive scholar and country squire, one of those who lived by their integrity and honor.

After the funeral, rather than return to the now empty Seaview House, O'Neill and I went to stay in Juan's Tavern in the village.

On the way, as we strode over the short trek, I asked O'Neill, "How did you come to realize that Miss Songana was the leading light?   She was only aided and abetted by Plumet who was a mere opportunist.   What about the suspicious, xenophobic locals in druidic beliefs and the bards?   At one time, I had even suspected the perpetually trembling servants.

"What about the dark-hooded monks striding vigorously all over the place; do they really have permission to walk and bless the land of locals?   Was this a good work on their part or just a fundraiser or was it something of a masquerade to hide their real hidden lives?   Were the monks right to fear pagan or sect rites?

"What of the rumors about the escaped convicts? What all did the precocious children, Cormac and Doreen, really know? What of the ghosts? Above all, who was the strange, ranting and raving guru in the village?"

O'Neill suddenly drew out two fivers and waved them at me.

"I'll tell you over dinner, old chap. All right? Dinner is on you, Garzon. See that's a tenner old boy. The five that you gave me and five interest that I have added usuriously since I gained the capital on false pretenses. This money should cover all our expenses at the hostelry."

I laughed delightedly.

"One of your little jokes O'Neill; you know you never borrowed from me in your life."

O'Neill's eyes blinked solemnly.

"I did not say borrow. I should have said begged."

"You begged from me, O'Neill, old boy? I don't understand."

Suddenly O'Neill straightened up to his lean, muscular, full height. His eyes stared. His hands were outstretched. He began to speak swiftly in an oriental accent.

"I say, give me the sacred lamp and the book of wisdom and I will find them a good home."

I shook my head in agony. "No. Oh no O'Neill, say that that wasn't you."

"Yes it was, Garzon. Still, our two fivers will get us a good meal at the hostelry here in Seaview village. There is a great dining room there with views over the high seas."

Little did either of us realize that those sea views were, in later years, to be the scene of one of our most horrendous and bloodcurdling adventures. Even the name of the tavern was prophetic.

In fact, we were to spend our time and the bogus guru's tenner at the inn which its Hispanic hosts had named, The Christopher Columbus.

Leaving our sticks, hats and coats with a waiter, we took up a table affording a fine view over the seas.

When we were seated comfortably, we were approached by Senor Gallegos. After mutual greetings we both decided to order our favorite meal of fish and chips with lots of mushy peas.

O'Neill leaned back, closed his eyes and stretched his arms.

"Welcome back, Senor O'Neill," said our Hispanic host. "Dear heavens, you have been following up some silly little mystery since you were a small boy and dressing up in disguise, a true actor. I saw your finger ring. It was worn by the mad ranting and raving oriental guru. Did you not remember the ring? It was so funny, Mister O'Neill."

We both joined Juan as he laughed. O'Neill did look incredulous for a moment then glanced at his quill and pen ring. O'Neill slipped off the ring which I had never noticed before. Sure enough it was a unique one displaying the tools of the auditor's or the writer's profession. Now the joke was on O'Neill as well as on me.

"Several folks in the village who have known me since boyhood including Juan here, our innkeeper, must have recognized me Garzon. I suspected as much. Why do you think they were so amused by my performance?

"Miss Songana was puzzled and afraid, not quite sure of my reality and terrified at the thought. Real Orientals come in so many shapes, sizes and colors that it's hard to be sure who is who. Many Indians, for instance the civil service classes, speak only English."

I shook my head, "I'm lost, but O'Neill you promised to tell me how you knew that Miss Songana was the queen of delusion."

"As clear as sunbeams my dear Garzon. No one had any motivation except Songana. Plumet was later motivated to kill us all for profit but the initial murder of two innocents was clearly the work of perverts.

"Garzon, just ask yourself about her strange nature. Playing wild, undisciplined music? Reading from a strange book by the light of a sacred lamp? An unbalanced temperament? Apt to fly off the handle? Taking human and flower and animal life very lightly?"

"Really, I'm amazed O'Neill at your perspective."

"Think about it, Garzon. Asking you to murder her co-conspirator? Killing innocent critters for no reason?

"The only person in common with both of the child killings was Miss Songana. My photos of the text, later translated for me, confirmed the deviant teaching of the book. I always suspected the innocence of the beggar in the first child murder. It would have been unusual for him to have had such a dedicated following if he had been guilty."

"Oh yes, I see it all now, O'Neill, she was studying an enigmatic book. It proved to be wicked in intent with doctrines of demons. But explain to me, O'Neill, the significance and the symbolism of the dead birds at the great oak."

"As clear as sunbeams again, my dear chap. The basket was poisoned of course and intended for me, a strange guru who was demanding her sacred lamp and book of wisdom. An eastern stranger was bound to be hungry so she thought and promised me the food to be left at the great oak. Remember, poison was her stock in trade. Unluckily I wasn't able to confiscate the poisoned food before a few of our fine feathered friends succumbed."

"What a deep and deceitful creature she was," I whispered, scarcely believing the truth.

"Well, the incident of the dead birds helped to save the lives of our household for, having the remains of the food analyzed, I found traces of the same obscure oriental poison that we now suspect had previously murdered both the children in her care. And of course, as attempted murder in itself, it established proof of her deadly intents."

"Well, O'Neill, your playacting as a guru was not in vain. You certainly alarmed and panicked her into the open."

O'Neill assented and explained that early on he had been quite suspicious of the sacred lamp and the book of wisdom as being worse than merely unorthodox.

"I suspected the book and lamp tended towards secret wisdom and dances with devils," O'Neill told me. "To me that meant one simple thing, total unpredictability."

As O'Neill explained it, that was why he had asked me to distract the governess while he photographed the sacred writings. It was then that he had gone to the Capital, to have those writings translated.

O'Neill continued, "Among all the tales of clashing spiritual forces of good versus evil, I was able to find many legends of a mystical lamp of enlightenment - a sacred lamp, coming from the high white hills of the Himalayas and the Russias, lair of the Yeti, the Abominable Snowman.

"These tales had drifted down to the Silk Road of the near east and into the jungles of India, Indo-China, China and the Eastern Isles of Nippon. These legends were connected with philosophies and creeds of the far north and the great orient."

"So O'Neill, let me try to get this straight. This Yeti religion, seeking hidden wisdom, is moving sinisterly through the deepest jungles and snows of the Far East and has now been given a second chance of survival. I have to ask, what indeed is wisdom and how do we come by it? Who has wisdom? Seek it and sell it not, says an old proverb. What do we know, O'Neill? Surely the lamp did not have magic powers to elucidate words of wisdom in the book?" I asked.

"Who can tell?" O'Neill replied, "Miss Songana was murderous but not stupid. She was prepared to risk her life for the book and lamp. Indeed, for those valued artifacts she lost her life and the life of her infidel admirer and companion in terror. Book and lamp demanded death sacrifice of children as the price of success. No doubt the followers of the Yeti had some strange reason, some experience or some weird coincidence at least that supported their belief."

"But what belief exactly?" I asked, still puzzled.

"Well, old chap," said O'Neill, "many believe that only spiritual powers can open up opportunities in this life. Many humans spend their entire lives totally dedicated not to succeeding themselves for that would be good but rather to tearing down and destroying the work of those who try to build and create. They must destroy even if they destroy themselves or wipe themselves out in the process. You see there is across all nations a strongly held belief, Garzon, that the world is a war between makers and breakers."

"Let us hope that makers must win in the end," I said sincerely, "and perhaps we can help them. The trouble is," I admitted, "finding out who is who. Who is make and who is break?"

"That is why solving such mysteries is so important," agreed O'Neill. "As for their written testament describing the powers of good and evil, they had no doubt many copies. However, the lamp and the book of wisdom which were stolen by Miss Songana were ancient and venerated artifacts, indeed icons.

"In all this she would have been instructed by her gurus or spiritual advisers. One of these had been her own late father. Having once attained an exalted position among the followers of Yeti, the Abominable Snowman, I do not wonder that her fanatical instincts broke out at least at times.

"The ugly counter-melodies that she played at times on the piano with her left hand was an omen. If it had been followed by the true melody or omen on the right hand this was considered, superstitiously, to be an indication that all would go well."

I nodded significantly and agreeably, my understanding of sonics not being quite up to O'Neill's musical expertise.

Changing the subject, I asked, "What were the real Orientals doing when they were seen by old Harry?"

"Yes," replied O'Neill, "you mentioned that the old coachman disturbed and drove away the presumed killers lurking about and hiding among the bushes in the morning. You are wondering what they were doing? I am very much mistaken if they were not trying to dig a grave for Plumet and the governess, for it is quite opposed to their usual customs to kill without having some receptacle prepared for the bodies.

"It was believed that the various colonial authorities had stamped out the followers of the Yeti to a great extent. However, it is unquestionable that the adherents of the Snowman flourish far more than the authorities suppose."

I was dazed with all of O'Neill's detailed research and shook my head.

Truly the dark places of the earth are full of cruelty and nothing but the light of the gospel will ever effectively dispel that darkness. That darkness will certainly not be dispelled by the stolen lamp which the priestess Songana stubbornly refused to give back to its rightful owners.

O'Neill added thoughtfully, "Apparently her Anglo-speaking mother's influence was strong on her education so that she did not fully agree with either her father or mother. In that case her mind was probably in turmoil at times and was split between occident and orient."

"I see it all now, O'Neill. The search for the lamp by the Orientals no doubt explains the various ghostly night visits to Miss Songana's haunts.

"Realizing the danger from the Yeti devotees, Miss Songana hid the lamp to which she also attached superstitious importance. After the poisoning and fire she planned to flee with it along with the bribe from Plumet. The Yeti fanatics lurking in the district realized her plan and foiled it to prevent her and Plumet making off with the Yeti's most valued treasures."

"Yes precisely, Garzon," said O'Neill, approvingly, "and I'm afraid I encouraged you to go for long walks with Miss Songana while I photographed dozens of pages of verses from her book of wisdom. While I pretended to carry out vague photographic experiments I was developing and printing those extracts. When they were translated, they had pointed so clearly to human child sacrifice as a path to spiritual success.

"That is why I went to the Capital. That was the urgent business. I contacted Jean-Baptiste Pierre, the great Anglo-French orientalist who translated the extracts for me. From these I found that Miss Songana was studying a book that advocated child sacrifice to appease the powers of darkness and thus attain spiritual strength to accumulate wealth and power at least in this world.

"Plumet had an extensive knowledge of the eastern languages and no doubt he also discovered the same as Pierre. This led him finally to conclude that she had murdered the second child in her care. Garzon, you were eventually able to figure this out."

Then I saw it all so clearly. It was so simple now that O'Neill had explained it. There was no longer any mystery about Miss Songana. She was a priestess of Yeti, pure and simple.

O'Neill continued, "Plumet saw that he could use this information in the cause of his own greed for wealth and prosperity. Truly greed is the most dangerous thing in the world, closely followed by stupidity. Indeed stupidity and greed are invariably a fatal combination.

"And as you once rightly noted, Garzon, Plumet was only superficially smart aleck but stupid really. He blackmailed Songana and forced her to join with him in the deadly plot against my uncle to take over his family home from which fate you valiantly saved us."

"I only followed your orders, O'Neill."

"Still, you saved Uncle Conn and my two young cousins from a cruel, painful death by a ruthless governess intent on obtaining dark insights. No doubt she was able to use those secret methods to ensnare your emotions. You had to make a big effort to do what you did, old chap, so deadly were her charms. And not for one moment do I underestimate your integrity and your moral courage."

I agreed miserably, "Yes O'Neill, I was bewitched by a witch. I feared that she was the victim of mesmerism but I must confess, dear chap, that I did have a soft spot for her at one time. However, my fascination somewhat faded when she demonstrated her savage and furious hatred for Plumet. That was a little more than I was able to deal with. She wanted someone to murder Plumet.

"Ah yes, how could I have been so deceived by a lady of spiritual power who was little more than beautiful in a land famously full of beautiful women?"

I felt that I had been in a very dangerous place, rescued only by my friend's research and analytical skill. Of course our combination of loyalty, quick action and dependability on my own part and O'Neill's sharp mind and analysis was to prove powerful in the future.

"I feel like a real fool, O'Neill," I stammered.

"Well, aren't we all fools at times, dear chap?" said O'Neill kindly, adding with a sigh, "you know, Garzon, that's what makes our Homo self-styled Sapiens, the most misnamed species of all."

The aroma of our meal drifted from the kitchen and then it arrived on our table. We stopped our pontifications temporarily as we tucked into our well deserved meal.

CHAPTER TWENTY SIX
A Matter of Conscience

O'Neill and Garzon discuss some legal and philosophical aspects of the case. They disagree somewhat but O'Neill makes a strong case for some very unorthodox opinions.

I could not help smiling at O'Neill's wit and felt a little better but not much. O'Neill was shrewdly glancing at me with a brief up and down survey then he grasped my elbow and pressed it.

"But O'Neill, surely the philosophy in the book of wisdom was not proof of her evil intent. It could have been mere fantasy."

O'Neill shook his head, "Remember the murder of the little girl whom Songana tutored in Sailport. Once murder walks and stalks, the scene ceases to be fantasy. Murder is for real.

"Then I uncovered the fact that the confession of that first child's murderer was totally false. He admitted as much when I confronted him in jail with the fact of the second child's death. Then tragically the false confession of the convicted murderer allowed the real killer, Miss Songana, to remain free to murder again. Those who falsely confess to a crime commit a double infamy."

I was astonished. "So the mendicant was mendacious," I responded.

The jingle seemed to pop up naturally from my tired mind and later suggested to me a name for this Felix O'Neill Case, 'The Mendacious Mendicant'. However, I later decided instead that 'Oriental Governess' was more appropriate.

O'Neill nodded. "Beggars often are liars because lies are their stock in trade. A groveling trickster confessed to the murder of a child. The sly beggar was innocent and so no one suspected Songana, who then killed another child.

"It is an outrage worthy of the most rigorous punishment to claim to have committed a crime of which one is innocent. Indeed, to make a false confession is a hideous offence against humanity."

I thought about this enigma. It was beyond me.

"Yet a person," I observed, "may be acting under severe torture or be a weak-minded person by nature."

"Possibly," agreed O'Neill, "but severe torture or the framing of halfwits is rare in these cases if not totally nonexistent. The police realize that confessions coming from a bruised and battered or simpering halfwitted self-confessor are unlikely to secure a conviction. Judges want to please the powerful in society. It's as simple as that. Even moronic juries, like mere mobs, think of their own place in the world and their social status.

"Therefore, in most cases there must be credible confessions but the problem is that such confessions may be signed by persons who merely wish to escape the temporary inconvenience and minor pain of aggressive interrogation.

"There are also those who confess because they are quite happy to live in jail and be fed and protected at public expense. There may be rare exceptions along the lines you suggest, old chap.

"Nevertheless, in general I cannot feel sorry if such persons should suffer the full punishment that is due for the crime to which they falsely confess. These are crimes which they have confessed to so selfishly in order to avoid the mere unpleasantness of the moment.

"These crimes will then be proliferated. Such persons are often offered exemption from hanging in return for a confession which is, in fact, being obtained by bribery."

"Really O'Neill," I cried, "I am quite confused. You are a hard, keen-minded man who would never break down but truly you should have more compassion for those who are of a weaker mental disposition. After all, O'Neill."

O'Neill shook his head and broke in quite acidly. "After all nothing, Garzon."

O'Neill took out his sharp pencil and pointed its thin end at me. It was a sure sign that he was upset when he resumed his former role as an auditor.

"Before you ramble on about being understanding, my compassion is for the victims of crime, not its perpetrators. I reiterate that a false confessor should receive the punishment due for all the crimes that were committed as a direct result of his false confession."

I nodded thoughtfully as I tried to take all these abstract ideas on board then, stalling for time, asked, "Do you know if there will be exhumations and autopsies of the dead children and has the innocent man been released?"

"That is all a matter for the Home Secretary, Garzon. It may take some time to resolve since there is no real proof of Songana's guilt. The lying beggar's release may never happen for all that I care."

"But O'Neill, surely we are speaking of an innocent person who may have been bullied?"

"No my dear Garzon. Really, can I not get it across to you that someone who sets a real murderer free to kill until caught, is not an innocent but rather a person who is merely utterly selfish and self-indulgent? Here is someone who is happy to set loose a predator, a murderer on the face of the earth to be free to continue his or her murders or other deprecations against all and any. How can you favor this?"

"O'Neill, I have never suggested such an immoral thing."

"Garzon, can't you understand that signing a false confession is a serious crime that has the devastating effect of setting the real criminal free?"

"Well, I suppose you are right, O'Neill, when you put it like that but I never thought of it in that way."

"Exactly, that is why I am concerned more with natural justice than with the law. As a great writer once wisely remarked, 'the law is an ass, whereas natural justice saves lives."

"Let me get this straight, O'Neill, the convicted killer was a weakminded liar who had falsely confessed. The import was obvious to you. The coincidence of two unrelated child murderers in two different locations was too great. It was obvious that either the governess or someone close to her had poisoned the children since there was no evidence of a third party being present at either murder scene. The overwhelming probability was that Songana, student of hidden wisdom, was an adherent of child sacrifice. Is this it?"

O'Neill nodded his approval. "That is it in a nutshell. Very well summarized."

"Thank you, O'Neill, but personally I would never care to make judgments based on ethical or religious concepts of natural justice. I would prefer to go simply by the law - much easier, of course."

"Yes, much easier but much less satisfactory. Law does not always cover the subtleties of individual cases. Too often the innocent suffer and the guilty go free or are even rewarded, all quite legally. Only natural justice, the basis of all codes, fills the gaps between the sparse keen teeth of the law."

O'Neill was unparalleled in his love of sword and harp. His brilliance of logic combined with music and morality amazed me, dazzled me.

For example, until that moment I had considered false confessors as victims of an overbearing system which is, of course, the picture presented by their supporters and advocates.

However O'Neill, with his rapier-sharp logic, unrivalled humanness, sympathy and fairness, foresaw the future. He thought of the inevitable victims of the false confessor. He knew that such a confession is bound to bring devastating destructiveness on the innocent victims of the freed-murderer's rampages. The mind of O'Neill was not just a sharp razor of logic but a clear cascade of the fresh water of fairness.

I saw that O'Neill's mind and judgment were of such a high order that he could well afford to raise justice above law.

He left me with some very important unanswered questions which I have never been able to really fathom.

Can we depend on judges, juries and police to convict the right person? If the wrong party is convicted and our law sets loose the real villain, is our legal system one of the reasons for our rising crime?

Certainly it looks like the world badly needs another Felix O'Neill to redress such wrongs. Can one really blame the followers of the Yeti for wanting to recover their stolen book and lamp or to avenge the treachery and greed of the beautiful governess?

People benefit from their clubs and churches and should be loyal to those who help them. Those disloyal to the state are executed. Is not the state supposed to be a model for others? Does the state set a good example?

"I wish I had your intellect, O'Neill," I remarked. "I have not read a healtharian book for several days and if I fail to ever complete my research I shall blame you."

O'Neill scribbled and doodled on a napkin with his sharp pencil, then laughed in a friendly way, "Nonsense, you are certain to succeed as Uncle Conn often used to say."

"You make a brilliant healtharian. You are nobody's fool for long. You have a good mind, Garzon, though it does not always operate - we must admit - like greased lightning. Yet, slow but sure is far better than fast and false. Everything worthwhile is always more difficult, costs more and takes longer than we had planned. Your researches are no exception and you must win in the end, dear boy."

Fighting back a lump in my throat, I responded, "It's damned decent of you to say all that, O'Neill."

It was the greatest compliment I have ever received in my entire career. I was overwhelmed.

I was glad to join in O'Neill's laughter. We were both of like mind and shared the same fears and hopes.

Well, Mr. Felix O'Neill is always right. I should say almost always and on this occasion yes, O'Neill was right as usual, I am very pleased to say.

CHAPTER TWENTY SEVEN

Afterword: On Destiny

Garzon returns to the Capital to complete his research and publish articles in distinguished journals. He comments nostalgically on the effect which this case was to have on their subsequent personal lives and careers.

I have little more to add to this terrifying case of the sacred lamp and Yeti, the Abominable Snowman. If I have been somewhat longwinded in the telling of it, I feel I owe no apology for that. I have simply set the successive events down in a plain unvarnished fashion and the narrative would be incomplete without any one of them.

However, I would like to say a brief word about the long-term consequences and aftermath of these horrific events that were shared by Felix O'Neill and your faithful, careful narrator, Arturo Garzon.

After O'Neill had solved the mystery of the oriental governess in the Celtcountry, I took the long train journey back to the Capital where I completed my research activities.

The events of this very difficult case destined me for a life as a healtharian researcher and O'Neill to continue his lifelong career of solving mysteries, whether practical or theoretical or historical.

If O'Neill had not gone to the Capital and investigated the case of the oriental governess, he and I would have no doubt perished unawares in the flames of the old house.

Truly our paths are set in this world by forces that seem to be just a little ways beyond our control. These are paths that are seemingly rehearsed in the great eternity that lies before and after us or perhaps alongside of us. I certainly make no claim to understand it in any way.

In any case, my perseverance and loyalty has made me a conscientious healtharian. On the other hand, O'Neill's originality and logic from its humble beginnings in double-entry bookkeeping, has made him something more outstanding, more distinguished than any accountant, auditor or economist. He has become the world's leading consulting detective.

THE END

Beware of the Ominous Visitor from afar